#38 in the TRIXIE Belden Series (handwritten)

DATE DUE

AUG 30 1986		
SEP 4 1986	MAR 5 1990	SE 1 3 '0
OCT 18 1986	SEP 22 1990	MA 06 '0
NOV 21 1986	MAR 20 1991	
JAN 13 1987	SEP 25 1993	
APR 21 1987	C-9-95	
MAY 20 1987	OC 10 01	
OCT 26 1987	SE 30'02	
FEB 27 1988	FE 9'05	
OCT 22 1988	MR 16 05	
JUL 8 2 1989	SE 04 '09	
AUG 2 1989		

F
J   Kenny, Kathryn
       Trixie Belden, The Indian
Burial Ground Mystery

FILED ON SHELF UNDER
CAMPBELL, JULIE

TRIXIE BELDEN

The TRIXIE BELDEN Series

TRIXIE BELDEN®

THE
INDIAN BURIAL GROUND
MYSTERY

By Kathryn Kenny

Black-and-white illustrations by Jim Spence

A GOLDEN BOOK • NEW YORK

Western Publishing Company, Inc., Racine, Wisconsin 53404

Copyright © 1985 by Western Publishing Company, Inc.
All rights reserved. Printed in the U.S.A. No part of this book
may be reproduced or copied in any form without written permission
from the publisher. GOLDEN®, GOLDEN & DESIGN®, A GOLDEN BOOK®,
and TRIXIE BELDEN® are trademarks of Western Publishing
Company, Inc. Library of Congress Catalog Card Number: 84-82558
ISBN 0-307-21561-X/ISBN 0-307-61561-8 (lib. bdg.)

Contents

1 * The Archaeologist

"WELL," Trixie sighed gloomily, "I guess I won't have to worry about my summer job. I just know I flunked the math final, so I'll probably be in summer school."

"Trixie Belden!" snapped her dearest friend Honey Wheeler with mock irritation. "If you tell me you failed the math final one more time, I'm not going to talk to you until we get our grades. You know perfectly well you never fail anything."

"There's always a first time," the sandy-haired, fourteen-year-old said mournfully as they walked up the driveway to Crabapple Farm, where the Belden family lived.

There were only a few more days of school left, and the two girls had been trying to line up summer jobs. It was going to be easy, though. In past summers, Trixie and Honey had volunteered as candy stripers at Sleepyside Hospital, and they expected to work there again this year.

"What do you think Mart and Brian will do this summer?" asked Honey, trying to get off the subject of the math final as tactfully as possible.

"They're looking for part-time jobs," Trixie replied.

Mart and Brian Belden were Trixie's older brothers. Brian, the oldest of the Belden children, was a junior at Sleepyside Junior-Senior High School. He was serious and hard-working, and he planned to go to medical school after college. Mart was Trixie's "almost twin." He was only eleven months older than Trixie, and he loved to tease her. Bobby was the baby of the family.

The blond-haired six-year-old came running down the driveway to meet the girls. His cheeks were rosy from the heat, and his eyes were glistening.

"What took you so long?" he gasped. "Moms says that you and Honey have to go straight over to the Manor House. I'm going to make my own garden. Reddy and me started working already." Reddy was the family's Irish setter.

"Why should we go to the Manor House?" Honey asked, bending to plant a kiss on Bobby's damp, curly hair. "Is there a problem?"

"I don't know," Bobby chortled. He spun around in the driveway and began a little hopping dance. "Reddy and me dug a big hole today. Moms says I can grow my own garden because Reddy cleared away the vines for me. You wanna help?"

"Of course," Honey said with a smile.

"But first," Trixie interrupted, "we'd better get over to the Manor House and see what Miss Trask wants. Wait for me while I drop off my books, Honey. I'll be back in a flash."

Trim, middle-aged Miss Trask had been a math teacher at Honey's boarding school until the Wheelers bought the Manor House in Sleepyside-on-the-Hudson. They'd hired Miss Trask to be Honey's governess. When Honey got too old to need a governess, Miss Trask became the manager of the Wheeler estate. Since the Wheelers traveled frequently, the arrangement worked out perfectly. She was cheerful and efficient—and Honey adored her.

Trixie dashed up the driveway of Crabapple Farm, past the row of crabapple trees and the fenced-in garden. The two-story, white farmhouse nestled comfortably in a wooded hollow. Hurrying up the porch steps, she dropped her books on the glider, then turned to run back.

"Trixie?" a melodic voice called from inside. "Is that you?"

"Yes, Moms," Trixie answered.

"Did Bobby give you the message?"

"Yes, he did. I'm on my way."

"Don't stay long. I need your help in the kitchen tonight."

"I'll be back as soon as I can," Trixie called over her shoulder. Then she launched herself off the porch and started back. Honey and Bobby were scratching letters in the dirt when she came up to them. By now, Trixie was panting and red-faced. Sighing at how cool and collected Honey looked with her shoulder-length, blonde hair and her crisp blouse and skirt, Trixie ran her fingers through her short, untameable curls. But it wasn't much use.

"You were probably born neat," she groaned as Honey straightened up. "You never, ever look messy the way I do."

"First of all, you don't look messy. And second of all, I didn't just run up and down the driveway in this heat," Honey answered with a laugh. "Ready?"

"Willing and able," Trixie replied. "See you later, Bobby."

"I wonder what's going on?" Trixie asked as the two girls quickly walked along Glen Road and up the long, winding driveway to the Manor House.

"I don't know," Honey answered as the elegant mansion came into view, "but it looks as if someone is visiting."

Trixie and Honey glanced at the unfamiliar station wagon parked in the circular driveway, and then bounded across the veranda into the spacious front hall. There were voices coming from the living room.

"Come on in, girls," came the booming voice of Mr. Wheeler. "I'd like you to meet someone."

Trixie and Honey slowed down to a sedate walk, and entered the huge, luxurious living room. Mr. and Mrs. Wheeler were seated on the sofa facing a stocky, balding man wearing a tweed jacket. A friendly smile creased his face when he saw the girls.

"Victor," Mr. Wheeler said proudly, "this is my daughter Honey and her best friend Trixie Belden. Honey and Trixie, meet Professor Conroy."

"How do you do?" Honey murmured, nodding politely.

"And I want you also to meet my assistant, Charles Miller," Professor Conroy said. His voice was high-pitched and his accent British. He gestured toward the French windows.

Trixie and Honey turned to see a tall, gangly young man who looked about twenty years old standing stiffly at the side of the room. Although nice-looking, with even features and shaggy, brown hair, the young man didn't smile. Nodding glumly at the girls, he immediately turned his attention back to the painting hanging on the wall.

"Is that a Renoir?" he asked pointedly.

"It certainly is," answered Mr. Wheeler. "It's small, but I like it, don't you?"

"Lovely," Charles murmured. One corner of his mouth lifted as if he were about to smile, but when he caught Trixie looking at him, he quickly turned back to the gemlike work of art.

"Pleased to meet you," Trixie said sarcastically, after throwing a sharp glance at Honey. But Honey didn't seem to be paying attention. Trixie turned to the adults seated in the center of the room.

"Professor Conroy is an archaeologist who will be spending the summer here on the game preserve," Mrs. Wheeler was saying. "He's bringing a group of first-year graduate students for a real archaeological dig."

Trixie's eyes lit up.

"Really?" gasped Honey. "That's fantastic!"

"I think so, too," replied Professor Conroy. "Your parents have kindly consented to allow me to search for artifacts left by the Algonquin and Iroquois tribes."

"Here?" Trixie interrupted. "I didn't know there were Indians here."

"There were Indians all over this area," Professor Conroy said. "But I'm sure you already learned that in school."

Trixie blushed furiously as she remembered that she had, indeed, studied the Indians who had lived in the Hudson Valley. But somehow the notion that all Indians lived only in the wild West had persisted. She glanced behind her at Charles Miller, hoping he hadn't noticed her foolish remark. But he wasn't even listening to the conversation. Prowling restlessly around the beautifully decorated room, he appeared to be examining everything with great care.

"As a matter of fact," Professor Conroy continued, "I have reason to believe that there is an important Algonquin burial ground right here on the estate. Thanks to the Wheelers, my students and I will be able to study the tribal movements of the east coast Indians on this dig."

"How can you study tribal movements from a burial ground?" Trixie asked, puzzled. "I mean, all the Indians are dead."

Professor Conroy burst out laughing, and Trixie blushed. *Oh, woe. How could I have asked such a silly question?* she thought in anguish. But before she could get even more embarrassed, Professor Conroy explained.

"That's a good question, young lady," he said. "You see, each tribe had specific ways of decorating its belongings. For example, clothing, pottery, knife blades, beadwork, basketry, and pipe heads had special designs etched or worked in as decoration, or to give the things religious significance. When a member of the tribe died, his belongings were usually buried with him."

"This is the part I don't understand," Mrs. Wheeler put in. "What do decorations tell about movements?"

"Elementary, my dear Mrs. Wheeler. The tribes moved around from season to season, and they followed herds of animals, as well. As they traveled, they met other tribes. They traded goods or gave gifts. I can tell the difference between a Virginia Iroquois tribe's pipe head and an Ohio Valley pipe head."

"That means," Trixie burst out, unable to control herself any longer, "it's kind of like detective work!"

"Exactly," Professor Conroy said, looking very pleased with her. "That's just what I tell my students."

"So you can figure out who those Indians

were visiting," Trixie continued, "and who was visiting them."

"You are a very smart young lady," Professor Conroy said with an appraising look.

"She certainly is," Mr. Wheeler agreed. "One of the smartest young ladies in town. Both these girls are good students and excellent members of the community."

"Oh, Professor Conroy," Trixie bubbled enthusiastically, "I don't mean to be pushy, but can high-school students work on your dig, too? We have the summer off, and it would be the most fantastic experience. I just love mysteries and detective work."

Trixie suddenly stopped, and her hand flew up to her mouth in dismay. She'd done it again—started talking too soon, trying to get in on something she shouldn't have. She didn't even know Professor Conroy, and she didn't know a thing about archaeology.

"Actually," Professor Conroy said with a kind smile as he turned toward the Wheelers, "I was intending to ask if you knew any young people who might like to help out on the dig. There's a lot of tedious work that needs to be done. It doesn't necessarily require any experience or knowledge—just enthusiasm and a strong back."

On hearing these words, Charles Miller suddenly spun around with a look of shock on his face. His mouth opened and closed quickly. A deep frown furrowed his brow. Before he could say a word, Mr. Wheeler had started to speak.

"I'm quite sure both these girls would be delighted to help. As a matter of fact, I think all the Bob-Whites would want to pitch in. It's a wonderful idea for a summer job."

"There would be no pay, of course," Professor Conroy said, coughing gruffly. "But the work would have marvelous educational value."

"Oh, gleeps," Trixie and Honey said in unison, clasping their hands with excitement. "I can't wait to tell the others!" Trixie added.

Professor Conroy pulled himself up from his chair with a pleased smile on his face.

"You do that. I certainly hope they're all as nice and smart as you two are. Now, Charles, I think we must be going. We've taken up quite enough of the Wheelers' time for today."

Trixie's eyes narrowed slightly as she watched the young man's shoulders droop. He threw one last look around the magnificent living room, and for a moment, Trixie thought she saw a look of desperate longing cross his face. But it disappeared, and was instantly replaced by the same scowl he was wearing before. Glumly, he followed Mrs. Wheeler and Professor Conroy out into the hall.

Honey dashed over to the couch and threw herself down next to her father. While she excitedly thanked him for suggesting that the Bob-Whites work on the dig, Trixie watched the two men depart.

Then Trixie heard a low hiss.

"How could you ask a bunch of dumb high-school kids to join us?" Charles Miller was saying as the front door was opened.

Trixie strained to hear what Professor Conroy answered, but the door banged shut behind him. All she could hear was some harsh mumbling. Professor Conroy sounded very annoyed.

Moving quickly, Trixie crossed the room to the French windows, hoping to catch a glimpse of the men. Luckily, the windows were open onto the veranda, and she was able to pick up their faint voices.

"Try and behave in a civilized way, you young pup," Professor Conroy snapped as they went down the steps. "Getting this burial ground is a stroke of good fortune for me, in more ways than one. I can't afford to have you mess up my carefully laid plans."

Charles's shoulders slumped even further as he walked swiftly to the car. Trixie smiled happily.

Talk about stuck-up, she thought as she watched the car drive away. *At least Professor Conroy knows a smart person when he sees one. Charles Miller will have to get used to the idea that just because he's in college, it doesn't mean he knows everything!*

Turning away from the window with a satisfied look on her face, Trixie walked toward the front door.

"Won't you stay for dinner, Trixie?" Mrs. Wheeler asked.

"I think I'd better start home," Trixie replied. "Moms wants me to help her out tonight."

"Come for dinner tomorrow, then," said Mr. Wheeler. "You know we always like to see you."

"Yes," Trixie answered, waving good-bye, "that would be nice."

She skipped down the veranda steps thinking what a wonderful summer it was going to be. *An archaeological dig! Wait till I tell Mart!*

she thought happily. Then a slight frown flickered across her face as she thought about Charles Miller. He certainly seemed unpleasant, but Trixie didn't care. She wasn't going to let a grouch like him interfere with an exciting summer like this one!

2 ∗ A Change of Plans

"Moms!" Trixie wailed as she threw herself full-length on the comfortably worn sofa in the Belden living room. "I can't believe you won't let me work on the dig with Professor Conroy. I just can't believe it."

"I never said you couldn't, Miss Smarty-Pants," Mrs. Belden said with a wry smile as she watched her daughter's theatrical misery. Helen Belden had heard nothing but "dig, dig, dig" for the last four days. Even Bobby Belden had been forced to listen to Trixie's tales about how "wonderful" the dig was going to be. "I only said that you can't let them down at the hospital. You know they depend on their volunteers each year. I would be most distressed if a daughter of mine went back on her word."

"But, Mother," Trixie moaned, "I can't miss the dig. Brian and Mart will be there, since they'll be working only mornings at the Historical Society. And Honey's parents said she could join in, too."

"Well, perhaps you can work something out, Beatrix," Mrs. Belden answered. "But until you've spoken to Mrs. Beales at the hospital, I don't think you should make any plans."

Despite the fact that her mother had called her Beatrix—her real name, which she hated —Trixie brightened at the thought that it might be possible to arrange something. She'd do anything to work on the dig with Professor Conroy! Springing into action, she flung herself off the couch and ran for the telephone to call Mrs. Beales. Mart, who was lounging in an armchair and lazily scratching the top of Reddy's head, watched her scramble out of the room. The Irish setter's tongue lolled out happily with pleasure.

Honey was sitting quietly in the window

seat. "I hope she can work it out," she said with a shake of her head. "If Trixie can't work on the dig, I won't either."

"Brian and I can't help it if we arrange our lives properly," Mart called after Trixie. "We just have a knack for living well, I guess."

A faint Bronx cheer came from the hall, followed by the sound of the phone being dialed.

"She'll work it out," Brian said quietly. "All Beldens have a knack for living well."

"Perhaps," Mart sniffed loftily, "but some of us have a more developed sense of—"

"The ridiculous," Honey finished. "Trust Trixie to fix this one. Mrs. Beales always liked her best of all the candy stripers. By the way, Jim isn't changing his plans. He's still going to work at camp this summer. He says he wants the experience."

"But he has higher goals than we do," Mart said seriously. "After all, if he's going to start a home for orphaned boys after he gets out of college, he's going to need all the practice he can get."

Jim Frayne was Honey's adopted brother. The orphaned nephew of James Winthrop Frayne, he had been adopted by the Wheelers after Trixie and Honey had helped solve the mystery of his inheritance. That was the summer that Honey had moved to Sleepyside.

When Honey first came to Sleepyside she had been painfully shy and frail. But after being friends with Trixie for a summer, she was healthy and outgoing. Honey had convinced her parents to let her go to public school with all her new friends. The Wheelers were so pleased with the change in their daughter, they'd happily agreed.

Trixie, Jim, Honey, Mart, and Brian had formed a semisecret club—the Bob-Whites of the Glen. Jim had taught the Bob-Whites a special secret whistle. It was the bobwhite birdcall, and it had inspired their club's name. The club was devoted to helping others and to having fun. Diana Lynch and Dan Mangan were also members.

Di Lynch came from a wealthy family who lived in a mansion not far from Crabapple Farm. She was known as the prettiest girl in school, with her long, black hair and large violet eyes. Like Honey, Di had been very lonely until she was befriended by Trixie and the Bob-Whites.

Dan Mangan, the newest Bob-White, was the nephew of Bill Regan, the Wheelers' groom. He worked as an assistant to the Wheelers' gamekeeper, Mr. Maypenny, and lived with Mr. Maypenny in a cottage on the preserve.

Trixie and Honey were very special friends. They both wanted to be detectives, and they planned to open the Belden-Wheeler Detective Agency someday. The two girls made a good pair because they complemented each other. Trixie was quick-tempered and impulsive, while Honey was naturally cautious. Together, they had already solved several mysteries.

"Well, Di's excited about the dig," said Honey. "Her parents said she had to watch her twin brothers and sisters for only half a day. But Dan can't make it, so it's not so bad if Trixie and I can't, either. Since not all the Bob-Whites will be participating, it can't be a club activity."

"That sounds like a rationalization to me," Mart said.

Suddenly a whoop of triumph was heard from the hall, and Trixie came back into the living room seconds later.

"Mrs. Beales said we could work half a day," she shrieked happily. "We just have to start early—at 8 o'clock—and work until 1 o'clock. Whoopee! A whole half day for the dig!"

"Oh, I'm so glad," Honey said excitedly.

"Great!" Mart exclaimed, hauling himself out of the chair. "Which reminds me, I haven't eaten for at least an hour. Food!"

"How can he eat all the time and still look like a bag of bones," Trixie mused as she watched Mart amble off to the kitchen.

"His basal metabolism is out of whack," Brian snorted.

"That's not the only thing that's out of whack," Trixie chuckled happily. "But enough about him. Where's Dad?"

"Enjoying a few moments of peace with his wife out in the backyard," Brian answered. "But he left the newspaper, so I think I'll try to catch up on current events, if you don't mind."

"I do mind," Trixie said, playfully snatching the paper off the coffee table. "May I have a look first? Miss Wilson, one of the kindergarten teachers in the elementary school, asked me to do her a favor and cut out pictures of food that she can use for her class."

"She wants them to eat newspaper?" Mart Belden asked, incredulous. He had come back into the room munching on a hamburger.

"No, silly," Trixie said. "She wants them to make a collage of the basic food groups."

"Ah, yes," Mart said. "The five basic food groups—fast food, sweet food, carbonated food, pizza, and hamburgers."

Trixie didn't laugh, and continued to read intently. Mart's expression changed from one of devilish glee to pained annoyance.

"Nobody listens to me around here," he griped.

"Hey, guys," Trixie said slowly, "listen to this—'Gang Robs Westchester Mansions.' This news article says there's a gang of thieves hitting all the big mansions and estates in the area. The police don't have any clues or leads yet."

"Sergeant Molinson will catch them," Honey said firmly.

"That's right," Mart added between mouthfuls. "He always gets his man. Or rather, Trixie always gets his man."

Mart was referring to the fact that Trixie had managed to solve a few cases that had stumped Sergeant Molinson and the Sleepyside police department. The sergeant didn't like her interference, but even he had to admit that the clever fourteen-year-old had a nose for crime.

"I wonder . . ." Trixie mused.

"Uh-oh," Brian said with a chuckle. "Here it comes."

"I wonder about that Charles Miller," Trixie continued, oblivious to her older brother's remark. She turned to Honey. "The way he was looking at all the things in your living room. Why, he even asked if the Renoir was real."

"Oh, Trixie," Honey said calmly. "Everyone asks that question."

"I know that," Trixie said thoughtfully, "but he was prowling all over, looking at everything so carefully. Don't you think that was a little odd?"

"For once in your life, Trixie, you have the opportunity to work on a mystery with redeeming social value," Mart began in his usual pompous way. "You are going to delve into the mystery of prehistory. Hey, did you hear that? I'm a poet! The mystery of prehistory."

"Oh, Mart," Trixie moaned irritably, "be serious for once in your life."

"I *am* serious," Mart answered quickly, looking a little hurt. "Why, I could join the ranks of the great and the near-great. Just think of it—Shakespeare, Wordsworth . . . me!"

Delighted with his own wit, Mart giggled merrily, then turned and headed back to the kitchen.

"I must have more food," he announced. "Great art cannot flourish in a vacuum."

By now, Honey was doubled over with laughter. Trixie started to laugh, too.

"Well, maybe I was making a mountain out of a molehill," Trixie finally said. "But I'm not going to give up."

"I feel much safer now," Brian put in as he followed Mart into the kitchen. "Knowing that Trixie is around eases a lot of my irrational fears."

Trixie didn't like being teased by her older brothers, and it was with great self-control that she managed not to throw the pillow she was holding at Brian.

"Come over to our house for supper," Honey said. "At least we Wheelers appreciate you."

"I'll go ask Moms."

As Trixie and Honey wandered out into the backyard to speak to Mr. and Mrs. Belden, they ran into Bobby. His face was smudged with long streaks of dirt, and he was waving something triumphantly in his hand.

"I'm an arpyologist, too," came his happy voice. "Look, Trixie, I found a real, genuine Indian arrowhead. Dad said so!"

Trixie looked at the little piece of sharpened stone that Bobby held in his hand.

"Why, Bobby, you *did* find an arrowhead," she gasped in delight. "Honey, take a look at this."

Honey turned the beautifully shaped piece of flint over in her hands, marveling at its loveliness. "We could show Professor Conroy this arrowhead," she said.

Bobby reached out and snatched his possession from Honey's hand.

"No!" he said. "Don't give it to anyone."

"Don't worry, darling," Mrs. Belden said soothingly. "They wouldn't give away your arrowhead. I'm sure Professor Conroy will be able to find one of his own. But it is interesting."

"The fact that Bobby can find an arrowhead right in our backyard shows that there must have been Indians in this area years ago," Mr. Belden said.

"Professor Conroy is very smart," Trixie

told her father. "He's obviously chosen the right place for this dig."

"I'm putting my arrowhead away in a special place," Bobby said, and he ran into the house.

"Will you be working on the dig?" Trixie's father asked.

"Yes, Dad. I arranged it with Mrs. Beales at the hospital."

"Isn't it neat," Honey said happily. "A real Indian burial ground, right on the game preserve."

"That's right," Trixie said. Then she had a thought. "Neat—but creepy, too. What if there are ghosts?"

"Ghosts?" Honey laughed. "Don't be silly. There's no such thing!"

"Ooooeeeeooo," Trixie howled eerily. "We'll soon see, won't we?"

The two girls burst out laughing, and then Trixie asked permission to have supper with the Wheelers. Mr. and Mrs. Belden agreed. Then they watched the two girls hurry off down the footpath that connected Crabapple Farm with the Manor House.

"Well, I'm certainly glad they have something interesting to keep them occupied this summer," Helen Belden said when the girls were out of earshot.

"Maybe we can get through a whole two months without a mystery," chuckled Mr. Belden.

"Don't count on it, dear. After all, you know our Trixie. If there isn't a mystery brewing today, she'll make sure one starts tomorrow!"

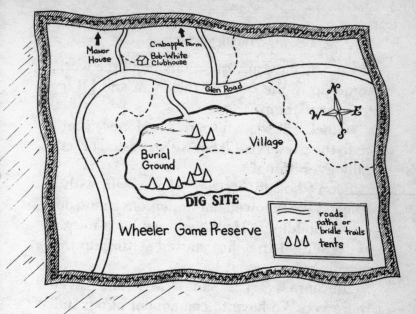

Manor House

Crabapple Farm
Bob-White Clubhouse

Glen Road

N
W E
S

Village

Burial Ground

DIG SITE

Wheeler Game Preserve

roads
paths or bridle trails
△△△ tents

3 * The Dig

THE LAST DAYS of school flew by, and Trixie didn't fail the math final, after all. Monday morning, Mrs. Belden dropped the girls at the hospital to pick up their candy striper uniforms and attend the first-day orientation meeting. The information was familiar to Trixie, but the new faces she saw in the group made her realize how important it was to know exactly what a candy striper should, and should not, do.

"All right, girls," Mrs. Beales was concluding, "tomorrow morning, bright and early. If

35

any of you have any questions about the work, come up to the front of the room and I'll try to answer them."

"Quick," Trixie whispered to Honey. "Let's go to the preserve. I'll bet we've missed practically everything!"

"Don't be silly, Trixie," Honey said with a laugh as she followed her impetuous friend out of the building. "How could we have missed everything if they just started setting up this morning?"

"Because," Trixie said, "we're not even there yet. We have to change out of our uniforms, have some lunch— Oh gosh, I can't bear the thought of missing even the littlest part! Don't you feel the same way?"

"I guess I do," Honey answered. "But it isn't driving me batty."

Mrs. Belden was waiting for them outside the hospital in the Belden station wagon. Bobby was firmly belted into the backseat and complaining loudly.

"I wanna sit *way* in the back," Bobby whined peevishly, "where you put the packages. It's more fun! Nobody would arrest a six-year-old for not wearing a seat belt. I think it's dumb. So there!"

"It's not dumb, Bobby," Honey said sweetly. "Look, I'm wearing my seat belt, and so is Trixie, and so is your mom. Smart people always wear their seat belts, and you're one of the smartest little people I know."

Bobby threw a grateful smile at Honey. Then, mollified, he settled down. The car drove swiftly along Glen Road. Mrs. Belden dropped Honey at the foot of the driveway to the Manor House, and then pulled into Crab-apple Farm. The moment the car stopped, Trixie bolted out the door and ran into the house.

"There are sandwiches on the kitchen table," Mrs. Belden called after her. By the time she had gotten Bobby and the groceries out of the car, Trixie had changed into shorts and a halter top, and was racing down the porch steps with a tomato-and-cheese sandwich in each hand.

"See you later, Moms," she called merrily as she jumped on her bike.

Trixie rode across the yard, and down the wooded path that led to the Manor House. Honey was there, waiting on the veranda steps with her bike and her sandwich. They quickly made their way along a dirt road to the part of the preserve where the dig site was located. A truck rumbled past them, kicking up clouds of dust.

"I bet it's a delivery," Trixie said. "Let's hurry."

Hot and out of breath, Honey and Trixie finally came to the clearing. It was a hive of busy activity. They could see tents being set up around the edge of the small meadow. Young people dressed in colorful shirts and shorts were carrying boxes, chairs, and stacks of books. Professor Conroy was moving tables and opening cartons.

"Brian," Trixie called out, catching sight of her brother. "Did we miss anything?"

Brian turned. Charles Miller was standing with him. They both had relaxed, happy expressions on their faces. Trixie wondered briefly why Charles appeared so nice when talking to her brother, and so prickly when talking to her.

Brian ambled over. "Don't worry, Trix," he said. "Professor Conroy is giving the opening lecture in about fifteen minutes. All you missed was the hard part."

"Good," the girls said, relieved.

"Hey," Trixie said to Brian, "what did you

think of Charles Miller? He's a little odd, isn't he?"

"Not at all," Brian replied. "Charles is extremely smart, and a real archaeologist. You wouldn't believe how much that guy knows about this area. When he heard I worked as a guard at the Historical Society, he immediately asked to see the archives. Charles says there's a wealth of original source material there—diaries, letters, all kinds of stuff. I'm going to take him down there as soon as he has some free time."

"That's very nice of you," Honey said, "but where is Professor Conroy going to give the opening lecture?"

"Oooh, that's right," Trixie said, her eyes sparkling with interest. "We should try and get front-row seats!"

"There are no front-row seats, silly," Brian said with a chuckle. "We'll probably all just sit around under a tree."

Suddenly the three young people heard a sharp noise. Turning, they saw Professor Conroy blowing comically on a little silver whistle. He was holding a sheaf of notebook paper in one hand.

With a wave he indicated that everyone

should join him under a group of shade trees at the edge of the clearing. Mart emerged from behind a stack of boxes and dashed across the clearing to join Trixie, Honey, and Brian. They quickly joined the group of ruddy-faced students. Trixie listened with rapt attention as Professor Conroy started to speak.

"Most people think an archaeologist spends all his time in remote regions of the world surrounded by missing links, dangling skeletons, and ancient, mysterious civilizations. Well, an archaeological site usually isn't as glamorous as people expect, but it can still fill one with awe. Here is where people actually lived their lives hundreds, or even thousands, of years ago.

"Archaeology is really the science of garbage—that's right, garbage. By going through the abandoned rubbish heaps of ancient civilizations, we can learn a great deal about them. We can find out how our predecessors lived, played, and worked."

Trixie looked around her. Suddenly the preserve that she knew so well came alive. She could almost see the Indians who once lived there.

The professor continued. "The Algonquin

and Iroquois tribes moved around in the Hudson Valley for hundreds of years. We are presently standing on what I believe is an Algonquin burial ground. Burial grounds are important because, in most tribes, a person's ritual objects were buried with him upon his death. Most of these things, such as baskets and deerskin clothing, have disintegrated over the years. But other things hold up better. These include knives, bowls, and pipes. Most of them were made of durable materials, such as bone, stone, or fired clay.

"It is these objects we are most interested in. Each tribe had specific ways of decorating their belongings. By comparing the decorative markings, we can try to determine the tribe's movements. On this dig, we're concerned with the tribes that moved along the eastern seaboard.

"Tobacco was grown and traded extensively in this region of the country. Much religious significance was placed on tobacco and its use, so the decorative markings on pipe heads were more formal and symbolic."

As Professor Conroy continued to talk about Indian rituals, Trixie listened, fascinated. When he was finished and began assigning tasks to each student, Trixie could barely contain her enthusiasm.

"Gleeps," Trixie sighed. "This is even more exciting than I thought it would be."

"Now, don't get too excited," Brian said reasonably, trying to calm Trixie down. "I doubt that they're going to let the high-school volunteers do the important work. After all, this dig is supposed to be for the graduate students. We'll probably be assigned to only the boring stuff."

"Nothing about archaeology could be boring," Trixie said in a rush. "Why, it's just like detective work. Sometimes the smallest, most insignificant clue is the one that solves the whole mystery! I almost think I'd rather be an archaeologist. What could be more exciting than uncovering the mysteries of the ancient past?"

"Well, you'll meet a better class of people," Mart put in. They were standing in front of a folding table, waiting to be assigned jobs. "No crooks, robbers, or madmen here. After an exciting life like yours, do you think you could stand the boredom?"

"Oh, Mart," Trixie said. "You know what I mean." She turned her attention back to Professor Conroy. He had been assigning most of his students to sections on a large map that lay on the table. The map showed the meadow where they were standing divided into numbered squares. A big, hand-printed label in bright-red ink said, BURIAL GROUND. To the east of the meadow was another, smaller area which was labeled, VILLAGE. While the professor assigned sections, a group of students were driving pegs into the ground and tying lengths of string between them, marking off squares just like the ones on the map.

The five Bob-Whites stood in line waiting to get their assignments. Di had finally located the group and was standing with them. She'd been delayed by the twins, who refused to eat their lunch, but she'd managed to arrive only a few minutes after Professor Conroy began his speech.

"Wasn't that exciting, Trixie?" Di whispered. "Oh, I hope I find something really terrific."

Trixie suddenly had a thought. She tapped the girl ahead of her on line and said, "Excuse me, but why are there two different sections to the dig? The map says 'Burial Ground' and 'Village.' "

The girl smiled in a friendly way, and gestured across the meadow toward a path that went off to the east, into the forest.

"Over there, in the woods, is the place where Professor Conroy thinks the original Indian village was located," she explained. "The meadow where we're standing was where the Indians buried their dead. He hopes to find most of the important artifacts here."

"Yikes," Trixie said, starting to hop from one foot to the other. "We're standing on graves!"

"We are not," Brian said calmly.

"Oh yes we are," she argued, her voice rising shrilly. "This whole meadow is the Indian burial ground. What if the ghosts of these Indians get angry and come back to haunt us?"

"That's what I love about you, Trixie," Honey began, trying not to laugh. But before she could finish, Professor Conroy was welcoming them to the dig, and assigning them to sections and jobs. Honey and Trixie were assigned to dig in the village site, which was in the woods. They were also asked to help out in the cleaning tent, which was at the burial ground site. Everything found had to be carefully cleaned with soft brushes and placed in marked boxes. Di had been assigned to the drawing group, because she was such a good artist. She was to make a drawing of each find on a three-by-five card. Later, the graduate students would try to date the finds based on where and how deep in the ground they'd been found. Mart and Brian were to help with the packing. Every find would be carefully packed in boxes to take back to the university for further study during the winter. Cataloging and classifying were saved for the more experienced college students. Each item would be identified by its shape and decoration, and then a large catalog would be made from the three-by-five cards.

"Whew!" Trixie said. "There's more to this than I thought."

Ghosts had apparently slipped from her mind. But she still walked carefully around the edge of the meadow as she and Honey made their way down the wooded path to the village site. All the tents had been put up, and the last of the equipment was being unloaded from the trucks.

The two girls were surprised when they got to the section of the woods where they were supposed to dig. It was deserted, dark, and forbidding.

"Who would want to set up a village here?" Honey said in a tremulous voice. "It's so gloomy. I would think that any Indian would hate it here."

"Honey," Trixie whispered to her friend, "look over there. What's that man doing?"

Honey turned to see a skinny, seedy-looking man pacing and whispering to himself. He would occasionally stop to jot something down in a notebook.

Honey thought she recognized him. "Wasn't he one of the delivery men? I wonder what he's doing off in the woods?"

Suddenly Trixie saw Charles Miller rush over to the man. Trixie and Honey, standing twenty feet away in the low undergrowth, could hear only snatches of their conversation. Charles called the older man Harry, and they seemed to know each other. Trixie put her finger to her lips, cautioning Honey to remain silent.

The two men spoke briefly, and Trixie distinctly heard the words "a real treasure trove," "map," and "historical society." Then Charles shook Harry's hand and said, "We won't have any problem dealing with those nosy kids. Just leave it to me."

When the two girls were finally alone again, Trixie was aghast.

"Did you hear that?" she whispered, her eyes as round as saucers. "He called us nosy!"

"How do you know he was talking about us?" Honey asked reasonably.

"Well, maybe not about us, but certainly about the Historical Society," Trixie said firmly. "He must have meant something about Brian! Remember, Brian said Charles was interested in the Historical Society. I'd better warn him that there's something fishy about Charles Miller!"

"Trixie!" Honey called after her disappearing friend.

But Trixie didn't hear. She raced back to the main area of the dig to find her brother. Honey followed her as fast as she could.

After Trixie had spoken to Brian, he made it clear that she was being much too suspicious.

"Charles Miller is a very nice, bright guy," he said. "Your mind is so full of crooks and mysteries that you seem to have lost the ability to see anything else."

"You like him because he cozied up to you, Brian," Trixie wailed. "Can't you see he wants to use you to get into the Historical Society?"

"Why shouldn't he want to get into the Historical Society?" Brian asked in his most rational tone of voice. It was the tone that often annoyed Trixie. "After all, he's a scholar. That's what scholars do—research in historical societies."

"Not to find out about archaeology and Indians, they don't," Trixie huffed back at him. Her hands were placed squarely on her hips as she defiantly faced her brother. "That's where a person would look for a treasure map—just like the one they were talking about!"

"Trixie," Brian said, his voice carrying a slight warning, "please calm down. I think you're on the wrong track. If it turns out you're right, though, I'll buy you a five-course dinner at the fanciest restaurant in town."

With that, he turned back to his work. Honey, who had been listening to the whole exchange, gently took hold of her friend's elbow.

"Come on, Trixie," she said. "It's 5 o'clock. Let's head back to the house. Maybe we can get Miss Trask to fix us some lemonade."

"I don't care if he doesn't believe me," Trixie muttered hotly. "I'll investigate on my own!"

"Not on your own," Honey said quietly. "Remember, I heard them, too. I'll help you. But in the meantime, let's assume they were talking about the buried treasure of archaeology, and a map of the dig site."

"I doubt it," Trixie said. "I really doubt it." The girls walked back to the main site, where they'd left their bicycles, then continued on to the Manor House.

4 ∗ Suspicions

THE NEXT MORNING, Trixie was ten minutes late leaving the house for the hospital. The girls had decided to ride their bikes to and from work each day, so Mrs. Belden wouldn't have to drive them. But Trixie missed Honey this morning, and had to ride her bike to town alone. She didn't catch up with her friend until 10 o'clock, when they were already on their rounds.

"Honey," she said in a loud whisper as they passed each other, "I have to talk to you!"

Both Trixie and Honey were pushing book

carts through the hall. Part of their job as candy stripers was to bring the little "libraries on wheels" to each patient. There were magazines, newspapers, and paperback books to choose from.

"I can't stop now," Honey said softly. "Is it important?"

"Of course it's important," Trixie said. "But I suppose I can tell you later."

"I'll meet you at 1 o'clock," Honey said, beginning to push her cart again. "I hope that's okay. It's just that there are so many floors in this hospital."

"I know," Trixie replied with a smile. "I guess the patients are glad to see us, because they all like to chat and then take hours to pick out a book."

"Three patients asked me to get them things from the gift shop," Honey said. "I'll be running around all morning!"

"Look," Trixie said, "I'll see you after we get off. It's *important!*"

The night before, as Trixie was falling asleep, she'd had a terrible thought. Maybe whoever had been robbing the Westchester estates—the ones she'd read about in the newspaper—were planning to rob the Manor

House, too. She was worried because Honey and Miss Trask were alone for the next month. Mr. and Mrs. Wheeler were away on a trip, and Jim was off being a camp counselor.

It was true that Regan was still home, but he didn't live in the main house. He lived in an apartment over the garage, which was separated from the main house by about fifty feet. Regan might not hear burglars if they came snooping around late at night.

At 1 o'clock, the girls met on the front steps of the hospital. As they walked around to the bicycle rack at the side of the building, Trixie told Honey about her fears.

"For one thing," she was concluding, "there are strange people around and one of them is Harry—and he has a truck. It's a perfect set-up, don't you see? We did overhear Charles Miller and Harry talking about a 'treasure trove.' And you remember that Charles spent a lot of time examining the valuables in your living room. It all adds up."

"It does and it doesn't," Honey said reasonably. "I don't think that Charles Miller is a burglar—he's a graduate student, after all. However, it's true that Miss Trask and I are alone in the house, and it's also true that people are being robbed. So I guess there is a *little* something to worry about. Maybe I should mention that article you saw to Miss Trask. She always manages to come up with a good solution."

Honey and Trixie pedaled their bikes along Glen Road as fast as they could. Splitting up at the Belden driveway, they agreed to meet on the dirt road in fifteen minutes.

Trixie rode home, changed into shorts and a T-shirt, had a bologna sandwich and a glass of milk, and climbed back on her bike. Pedaling as fast as she could, she met Honey, and they quickly made their way to the dig site.

The students and Professor Conroy were just finishing their lunch break. Professor Conroy, after carefully wiping his hands and his mouth, began another of his mini-lectures before they all got back to work.

"I love this," Trixie whispered to Honey as they sat down with the group. "I bet this is just what college is like."

"Now, before we begin in earnest," Professor Conroy said, rubbing his hands in anticipation, "I want to refresh your memories about how we dig. We don't, and I repeat *don't,* dig—we scratch! A pick or a shovel is too heavy a tool to use. Mark off a small section for yourself, and carefully scratch the ground away. You might come across a delicate pottery shard, and you don't want to break it. You also don't want to miss anything, so go slowly and carefully.

"If you find something, make a note of where you found it, and how deep down it was before you continue. And don't throw anything away. What looks like a rock to you could easily be a tool of some sort, or a pipe head encrusted with dirt. That will be the hard part for you, as it is for all of us. Trying to decide what is junk, and what is a junk-encrusted find, is something that torments all archaeologists.

"I thought I'd show you some pictures of standard pipe heads, so you'll see what the general shape is. The eastern tribes were the most frequent pipe smokers, and they designed a number of different pipes. One of them, as you can see here, has a flat, oblong base on which is set a round bowl. Because this style of pipe resembles the Civil War battleship, it has come to be called a monitor pipe. Other pipes have very tall bowls set at varying angles near the end of long, flaring bases.

"A pipe has the general shape of the letter L. This shape is not commonly found in nature. If you find something with this shape, check with the student head of the dig before you throw it away. I've assigned that position to Charles Miller."

"Oh, no. Not him!" Trixie groaned as Professor Conroy gestured towards Charles. Charles nodded his head and smiled.

"Now let's get to work," Professor Conroy concluded. "We all know what we're supposed to be doing, and where we're supposed to be doing it. Good digging—I mean, good scratching!"

Trixie and Honey trudged away from the beehive of activity at the burial ground site. They followed the path leading east through the woods, away from the busy meadow and the cheerful students, and finally found their section. Gloomily, they surveyed the area. The trees were tall, and closely grown. A thick mat of vines and briars made it difficult to walk around. Several large fallen tree trunks crisscrossed what little clear space there was to be found.

"I still don't get it," Trixie mumbled. "What a dumb place to make a village."

"Maybe it wasn't such an unlikely place five hundred years ago," Honey said. "We learned in geography that everything changes. What was once a meadow becomes a forest; what was once a lake becomes a meadow. Who knows, maybe this used to be a cozy little clearing."

"Well, it certainly isn't a cozy little clearing now," Trixie muttered. She sat down on a rock disconsolately. "What are we going to find around here anyway? Probably nothing but a few aluminum flip-tops from soda cans."

"They didn't have soda five hundred years ago."

"Honey!" Trixie choked out after a burst of laughter. "You know what I mean!"

The two girls were so busy giggling, they didn't hear the sound of approaching footsteps. As Trixie wiped tears of laughter from her eyes, she saw that Charles Miller was standing in front of her.

"What are you doing here?" he asked gruffly.

"W-we, uh, we're working here," Honey stammered.

"Well, I don't want you working here," Charles said, glancing around nervously.

"Wait a minute!" Trixie snapped, her hot temper getting the better of her. "Professor Conroy assigned us to work in this section, and this is where we're going to work."

Honey glanced at her friend in amazement. Only a few minutes before, Trixie had been complaining about this spot. Now she was defending her right to stay here as if she loved it more than anything in the world.

"Well, I'm the head of this dig, and I say you can't dig here," Charles told her. As he spoke, his face got red, and he rubbed his palms along the sides of his shorts.

Why, he's nervous, Honey thought.

"We'll just see about that," Trixie retorted. "I'm going to check this with Professor Conroy. C'mon, Honey."

Charles became more upset, and started to follow Trixie. Then he stopped in his tracks and called after her instead.

"I wouldn't bother him if I were you. You high-school kids aren't serving any purpose on this dig. We don't need you here at all."

Honey hurried to catch up with Trixie. Reaching out her hand, she touched Trixie's shoulders softly.

"Slow down a minute and catch your

breath," Honey said. "You shouldn't go storming up to the professor. Try to calm down."

Trixie realized her friend was right.

"In fact," Honey continued, "he may even assign us to someplace better. Sometimes these things work out for the best, you know."

Trixie took a deep breath. "I know that, Honey, but Charles made me so mad. He really shouldn't talk to us that way."

"No," Honey agreed, "but for some reason he doesn't want us working there. Once Professor Conroy reassigns us, though, we'll be with the other students and we'll make new friends. It's the best thing that could have happened."

"Maybe," Trixie said slowly. "But I've been thinking about it, and I'd rather work at the village site than, well, on the actual burial ground. What about the ghosts?"

"Trixie! You don't believe in ghosts any more than I do."

Trixie clapped her hand over her mouth. "Oh, rats!" she said, stomping her foot. "I left my pick and my sifter back at the village site. I'll be right back."

"But, Trixie . . ." Honey yelped.

"I'll meet you back at the meadow," Trixie

called over her shoulder. Then she set off running through the woods.

She was almost at the site, when she heard voices drifting through the trees. Slowing to a crawl, Trixie walked as quietly as she could, trying to catch a glimpse of who was talking—and trying to avoid being seen.

It was Charles Miller, and he was talking to Harry again.

"Make a date with that kid from the Historical Society," Harry was saying, his voice a low whine. "We gotta get that map, and we gotta get it in a hurry."

"I don't see why—" Charles began, but Harry cut him off.

"Take it from me, kid," Harry said, "we haven't got much time. You wanna fool around in the woods with a pail and shovel, be my guest, but—"

It was at this moment that Trixie, trying to creep closer in order to hear better, tripped over a gnarled tree root. With a cry of dismay, she sprawled flat on her face right in front of the two men.

"What the . . ." Harry snapped at the intrusion. "Who's that?"

"A troublemaker, that's who," Charles said

as he looked down at the disheveled girl. "Didn't I tell you to get lost?"

"I forgot my tools," Trixie explained lamely. She could feel herself blushing with embarrassment.

"Well, hurry up and get them, and then get out of here," Charles said, scowling at her.

Trixie scrambled to her feet and walked slowly across the tiny space separating her and Charles. She had to climb over a fallen tree trunk to get to the place where she'd left her tools. "Yes, sir. Your wish is my command."

I sound just like Mart, she thought as she quickly collected her things. Then, straightening up, Trixie looked defiantly at Charles Miller.

"If I were you," she said with a smug grin, "I'd try being a little nicer to people. Nobody likes a grouch!"

"Why you . . ." Charles started.

"Hey, do you think she was listening?" Harry snapped, his eyes narrowing as he watched her.

"I doubt it," Charles answered. But he looked a little worried. "It doesn't matter, anyway. For one thing, she's just a high-school kid.

And for another, I'm going to see to it that she gets thrown off this dig."

Squaring her shoulders and holding her head high, Trixie slowly marched away from the two men.

"We'll see about that," she muttered under her breath. "And wait until I tell Brian and Mart what I just heard. You guys won't get *near* the Historical Society if I have anything to say about it."

Filled with determination, Trixie hurried through the woods to find Honey—and Professor Conroy.

5 * Treasure Talk

"AND THEN Charles said we weren't allowed to work there," Trixie said to Professor Conroy, trying to control her anger. "We were working just where you told us, too."

Professor Conroy looked perplexed. Slowly turning a small trowel over and over in his hands, he looked at the red-faced girl standing in front of him.

"It really doesn't matter where anyone digs," he finally said. "I'll speak to Charles and see if there's any reason for this. In the meantime, why don't you go over to the students in the cleaning tent and see if they need any help."

Slightly annoyed that Professor Conroy hadn't exactly taken her side, Trixie stood there lamely, trying to hide her anger. Although Professor Conroy didn't say as much, Trixie detected an expression of annoyance on his face. She wished she could think of something to say that would make him go off and scold Charles Miller. Then, thinking better of it, Trixie turned away. After finding Honey, they spent the afternoon hanging around the cleaning tent, accomplishing nothing.

That night after supper, the Bob-Whites met in their clubhouse. The clubhouse had once been the old gatehouse on the Wheeler estate. The Bob-Whites had repaired it, hung curtains, and added some old furniture. They'd even gotten a wood-burning stove from Mrs. De Keyser, who lived down Glen Road. The stove made it possible for them to use the clubhouse for most of the year.

Trixie was curled up in a newly covered armchair. She had just finished telling Di, Mart, Dan, and Brian about the unfortunate meeting in the woods with Charles Miller and Harry.

"Maybe there's a *real* treasure buried on the preserve," Trixie concluded excitedly.

"I still say, Little Miss Detective," Brian said firmly, "the only thing Charles Miller could possibly be talking about is the buried 'treasure' of archaeology. You're wasting your time."

"I am not," Trixie countered. "I think Charles Miller and Harry know something about a real treasure. I say they're using this dig as a cover for finding it. Maybe they're looking for Captain Kidd's treasure."

"The only thing people find when they're looking for Captain Kidd's treasure," Mart said with a superior look on his face, "is *other* people looking for Captain Kidd's treasure."

"What about the map part?" Trixie asked. "What other kind of map could they be talking about in the same breath as treasure?"

"Probably an old map of the Indian encampment," Brian said reassuringly. "Now don't get yourself all worked up over nothing."

"Nothing!" Trixie blurted angrily, but inside she was disappointed that Brian didn't agree with her. He usually took her side, and Trixie was always grateful for it.

"Speaking of nothing," Mart interrupted, "I have had nothing to eat since dinner. What we need in this clubhouse is a refrigerator full of food."

"It's only been an hour since dinner, but let's all go to the Manor House," Honey suggested. "There's always loads of food there, and Miss Trask said she's missed us lately."

"I've missed her, too," Di said softly. "I've been so busy with the dig and taking care of the twins. I haven't had a chance to see anyone."

"Let's go," Mart whooped, skidding out the door. "No sense hanging around here talking about food. We could be up in the kitchen doing something about it!"

As the six young people trudged up the driveway, they heard the sound of laughter and music coming through the trees.

"That must be coming from the dig," Trixie exclaimed.

"It sounds like guitars and folksinging," Di said.

"It sounds like a party to me," Brian said. "Let's go see!"

"What about food?" Mart moaned dramatically, clutching his stomach.

"Forget about food for a while," Dan said. "Maybe we'll have some fun, instead."

"What could be more fun than food?" Mart mumbled as he grudgingly followed the other Bob-Whites along the dirt road leading to the dig site.

When they came to the clearing, a lively campfire was burning. The students were sitting around the fire on logs and rocks, singing and talking. Professor Conroy was there, too, and it looked as if a delightful songfest was on.

"Join us," he boomed, seeing the six Bob-Whites straggle in through the trees. "We need a tenor. Any of you a tenor?"

"At your service," Mart called back. Then he began to warble, "Do-re-mi-fa-so-la-ti-do!"

They all found spots in the circle, and the singing continued.

"Where's Charles?" Brian asked, after looking around the assembled group.

"He's in the city," answered one of the graduate students. "He goes there every night."

"Why?" Trixie asked with interest.

The girl replied with a toss of her long blonde hair. "He pays his own tuition, so he has to work every summer to earn money. But he didn't want to miss the dig, either. He decided to do both."

"How can he do both?" Di asked.

"He works on the dig during the day, and he has a night job, that's how. That way he earns the money, and doesn't lose the course credit."

"Whew," Brian said. "That's a rough deal."

Trixie suddenly had a thought. All the talk of Charles had stirred her questions again. Since she hadn't gotten too much sympathy from the others, she decided to talk with Professor Conroy. Maybe he would have a key to what Charles was talking about in the woods. Shifting her place, she managed to find a spot next to him around the campfire.

"You wouldn't happen to know any stories about treasure in this area?" she asked during a break in the singing.

"Oh, yes," Professor Conroy answered. His eyes started to glow in that special way they always did when he was about to begin one of his little lectures. "But there are always hundreds of treasure tales that circulate in areas of great historical significance such as this one. Why, I could go on all night.

"Ahem." He cleared his throat happily. "For example, Captain Kidd—whom you surely have heard about—is said to have buried various treasure caches along the Hudson River. There's supposed to be a cave somewhere around Crow's Nest—right near here—which contains some of his treasure. He was also supposed to have buried treasure on Gardiners Island, in Gardiners Bay, and on Long Island. But no one's ever found a bit of it. I can only assume that he never actually buried it. Maybe he spent it all, heh-heh."

Professor Conroy was obviously enjoying himself. "There are Dutch treasure legends, too," he went on. "With ghosts! A long time ago, a Dutch ship laden with treasure sank in the Hudson. The survivors knew where the treasure should have been, but because of shifts in the channel and shoreline of the river, they were never able to find it. But they swore to continue looking. Rumor has it that at low tide, when the moon is full, their ghosts still wander up and down in search of the gold, while a white hound howls at their shadowy wraiths."

By this time, the singing had petered out and the group around the campfire grew hushed. The professor's rumbly, eerie voice made the stories seem truly scary. Honey shivered. Trixie was sorry she'd even asked. She didn't really believe in ghosts, but still. . . .

"Ooooo Ooooooo," Mart wailed spookily. Trixie jumped as the others laughed. "Let's tell ghost stories around the campfire," Mart said.

"Let's not and say we did," Honey answered nervously. "Besides, it's getting late. I should be getting back home. We all have to get to work early tomorrow."

"Absolutely right, Miss Wheeler," said the professor. "We should all pack it in. Early day tomorrow for us chaps, too."

Everyone stood up, and while they were stretching, collecting guitars and cases, and pouring sand on the fire, Trixie seized another chance to ask Professor Conroy about Charles Miller.

"Why, yes, Miss Belden," he answered cautiously. "I did talk with Charles Miller about that little contretemps this morning. I've decided to have Charles supervise the work only on the burial ground. As student head of the dig, he should be spending his time on the most important area. The village site has far less significance—not that you girls should feel bad about being assigned there."

"But what about—" Trixie started.

Professor Conroy went right on talking. "Charles is an exceptional student—one of the best I've ever had. But he has money problems, and that sometimes makes him bad-tempered. I don't think you girls should worry about Charles. I'm sure he'll be around to apologize to you tomorrow."

Trixie nodded her head, but she felt wary. *Apologize? I'll believe it when I see it,* she thought glumly.

Noticing that the other Bob-Whites were saying good-night to everyone, Trixie quickly excused herself and caught up with them.

"There wasn't one speck of food at this gathering," Mart grumbled as they walked home. "I suppose it's too late to make a little side visit to your refrigerator, Honey."

"I'm afraid so, Mart," Honey said with a laugh. "Will you live?"

"I doubt it."

The group split up at the clubhouse, and Honey ran up her driveway. Dan walked Di back to her house, and then he went on to Mr. Maypenny's. The three young Beldens made their way home to Crabapple Farm.

As they walked, Trixie thought about everything she'd learned tonight. One thing stuck out in her mind—Charles Miller needed money, badly. Instead of calming her suspicions, that fact pointed to just one thing—Charles's guilt. *Graduate students aren't known for being burglars,* Trixie thought, *but most students aren't as poor as Charles Miller is, either. And then there was that mysterious conversation with Harry in the woods, and the newspaper article, and Charles's hostility toward her and Honey. It was all pretty suspicious—and pretty confusing, too.*

By the time they arrived home, Trixie was too tired to think about Charles Miller anymore. Slowly, she made her way up the stairs to her room, thankful that it was bedtime. Tomorrow would be another long day.

6 * A Mysterious Accident

WHEN TRIXIE got to the second floor of the hospital the next day, she made a startling discovery.

As she wheeled her book cart into room 204, the door started to swing shut. It banged against the side of the cart and a pile of magazines slid to the floor with a loud flap. She didn't see who the patient was until she stood up, holding the slippery pile in her arms—and then she almost dropped it again.

"Professor Conroy!" Trixie exclaimed. "What are *you* doing here?"

"I'm not sure I know," Professor Conroy answered. He attempted a weak smile, but his voice quavered. "Bump on the head, apparently."

"How did you bump your head?"

"That's the odd part. I got up last night to head for the bathroom, and the next thing I knew I was in here."

"What does the doctor say?" Trixie asked, appalled.

"Must have hit my head on a low-hanging branch or something. Might have a concussion. I'm in here for observation for ten days. Can't even get up. Terrible!"

"What about the dig?" Trixie gasped. "Who will take care of things?"

"Fortunately, I have Charles," Professor Conroy sighed. "I don't know what I'd do without him."

Trixie thought for a moment. An upsetting conclusion was forming in her mind. *Fortunately, my foot,* she thought. *I need to find Honey—and right away!*

"Would you like a magazine or a book?" Trixie asked quickly. "Can I get you anything at all?"

"No, thank you, Miss Belden," the professor

answered weakly. "I think I'll just lie here quietly. I don't know whether I'm supposed to read or not. The doctor said he'd drop by this afternoon and have a chat about my condition."

Trixie told Professor Conroy she'd check in on him the next day. Then she quickly pulled her book cart out of the room, and parked it in the corridor. She raced off to find Honey.

It was almost 1 o'clock when she finally found Honey sitting at the bedside of an elderly man, reading him the newspaper. Trixie controlled her urge to interrupt, and backed out of the room. In a few minutes, Honey would be through, and she could tell her everything on the way home.

"Don't you see?" Trixie said as they rode their bikes along Glen Road. "Charles didn't like being told to stay away from the village site. So he hit Professor Conroy on the head last night, figuring it would look like an accident. Now he's in charge of the dig for ten days, and he can do anything he wants!"

"I still don't see why Charles wanted us to move. What's the connection between the place where we were assigned to dig and a treasure? Besides, Charles was off at work last night."

"He could have come back from New York anytime. Or Harry could have done it."

"I thought you said Charles was a burglar. Burglars don't hit people on the head unless they get interrupted in the middle of a burglary."

"I'm sorry you don't agree with me, Honey. But I know there's something fishy going on, and I'm going to find out what it is."

The two girls rode on. Since Professor Conroy had told them to continue working at the village site, that's where they headed. But when they arrived, they found a very gloomy-looking Charles sitting on a log.

"Didn't I tell you girls to get reassigned?" he asked grouchily. "You keep turning up all the time, like bad pennies."

"Didn't he tell you?" Trixie started with a smug look on her face. "We checked with Professor Conroy last night, and he said that he'd told you to devote all your time to the burial ground."

"He never said a word to me about it," Charles replied.

"What?" Trixie asked, startled.

"Listen," Charles continued, "I'm student head of this dig, and I'm telling you to get reassigned."

Trixie was furious. Honey was perplexed. Both of them had heard Professor Conroy say he'd spoken with Charles. But Charles was denying ever having had such a conversation. One of them wasn't telling the truth, and it was probably Charles. But how to prove it? And what could be the reason for Charles's denial? Suddenly Trixie had an idea.

"All right," Trixie said with a conciliatory smile. "Anything you say. But we're worried about Professor Conroy. How did he get knocked unconscious in the middle of the night?"

"Unconscious?" Charles was visibly surprised. "He wasn't knocked unconscious. This morning he complained that he felt ill, something about allergies. He went off to see the doctor. How do you know he was unconscious?"

"Because he told me so in the hospital this morning," Trixie said, carefully observing Charles's facial expression. "The doctors think he might have a concussion."

Charles looked shocked, then mumbled

something about having to check into it later. He turned away from the girls, and began consulting a chart showing geological features and elevations of the preserve.

The girls said a hurried good-bye and went off to look for Brian.

"He's obviously lying," Trixie mumbled. She swatted a fly that was buzzing furiously around her face, and she couldn't resist making a joke about it. "You know, Honey, this forest is full of annoying insects. The six-legged *and* the two-legged kind, if you know what I mean!"

Stomping back through the woods was difficult. The air was hot and muggy, and it felt like rain. Both girls were feeling bad-tempered and confused. When they finally located Brian, he wasn't much help.

"I still don't feel any differently about Charles Miller," Brian told his sister. "Charles is a very nice guy. I spent the morning with him in the archive room at the Historical Society. I had a chance to watch him and talk with him. There's nothing strange about him, believe me."

"What was in the archive room that Charles Miller needed to look at?" Trixie asked sharply.

"Revolutionary War papers and books, for your information," Brian snapped back. But there was a small twinkle in his eye. "No maps, Trix, just diaries and letters and stuff like that."

"He's supposed to be interested in Indians, not the Revolutionary War," Trixie said in a sulky voice. "That's history, not archaeology."

"Not true," Brian said, tousling her hair. "You think the Indians disappeared the minute the settlers arrived? They ate Thanksgiving dinner and then said good-bye forever?"

"No. I guess not," Trixie conceded.

"There happens to have been a big overlap," Brian continued. "A lot of the letters and diaries written back then mention Indian customs, lore, and stories. Is that so suspicious?"

"Maybe not," Trixie said, but she refused to give up. "I'll have to do my own research. But I still say that Charles hit Professor Conroy on the head last night. He was angry at him, wasn't he?"

"Maybe he *was* angry at him," Brian said, trying to be patient. "But that doesn't mean he hit him on the head. We're civilized people, not a bunch of monkeys who go around acting out our aggressions. Sometimes I get angry at you, but I don't go banging you on the head, do I?"

"Brian, I wish you would take me seriously," Trixie said in an exasperated voice. "I would never accuse someone if I didn't feel I had good reason. You know that."

"This time I think you're wrong."

"We'll see," Trixie said. "If you thought about it, you'd know I was right."

Honey was surprised to see Brian and Trixie arguing like this. Usually the two were quite close. But neither of them would give an inch. Finally Trixie squared her shoulders and stomped off in a huff. Brian shrugged and went back to work.

Honey hurried after Trixie. "What are you going to do?" she asked.

"You'll soon see," Trixie answered. "I've got a plan."

Trixie pulled her bike from the bushes, and brushed a stray lock of hair from her face. "I'm going to the archive room."

"But why?" Honey asked.

"I want to see if I can find what Charles Miller was *really* looking for," Trixie said. "He may have my poor brother snowed, but not me. I bet he was looking for something specific—a map that shows where a treasure is buried. The guard will let me in because I'm Brian's sister."

"Aren't you going to change first?" Honey asked. She looked Trixie up and down.

"No," Trixie said wearily. "It's so hot that by the time I get to town, I'll just be all rumpled up again. Are you coming with me?"

"Of course," Honey answered. "I have to go into town anyway. Miss Trask asked me to pick up a book for her at the library. I was supposed to get it on my way home from the hospital today, but I completely forgot. While you're in the archives, I'll stop at the library and get the book."

The two girls pedaled along Glen Road, trying to keep close to the shaded edge of the road. The afternoon was uncomfortably hot. There was a gentle breeze, but it didn't do much to cool things off.

They finally reached the library, which was very near the Historical Society. Both were among the oldest houses in Sleepyside. Surrounded by huge oak trees, the buildings were cool even on the hottest days.

"Whoever gets finished first can come and get the other one," Trixie said as she and Honey parked their bikes near some shade trees.

"Will you be long?" Honey asked.

"Who knows?" Trixie answered grimly. "This could take hours."

The two girls went their separate ways. Trixie headed up the front steps of the beautifully restored Historical Society. Inside, she quickly found Jake Hanson, the guard. He was delighted to take her down to the archive room.

"Lotta renewed interest in history these days," he said as they went down the wooden staircase to the locked basement room. "Why, I think it's terrific that young folks like yourself are willing to take time to study these things."

Trixie nodded as she followed the stoop-shouldered, frail little man. He'd been the guard at the Historical Society for as long as she could remember. When she was little, she'd always thought Mr. Hanson lived in these quiet, old rooms—just another antique like the rest of them.

"Yessiree," he continued, opening the door

for her. "It's important to know your history. Now, you let me know when you leave, and I'll lock up after you."

Inside the archive room there were rows and rows of glassed-in bookshelves and display cases. A small, square wooden table with two matching chairs were in the center of the room. Lying open on the table was a small leatherbound book with a locking clasp.

Sliding into one of the chairs, Trixie pulled the book closer and took a look. It appeared to be someone's diary, and it was open to an entry dated January 3, 1777. Trixie silently read the pale, spidery handwriting. It said:

Although I have worked with all zeal to establish false proof of my regard for this infamous uprising, I have reason to fear that I will soon be unmasked. The recent declaration, or resolve, by the new illegal government gives me cause for fear. Aid and comfort given to any person allied with the rightful King George will result in the pains and penalties of death.

I intend to bury a sum of gold in a certain cave known only to me. In this way, should I be taken, these selfstyled patriots shall not have my family's fortune to aid and abet their grievous war against our sovereign. Should I survive, I will reclaim it. My only fear is that the privations of war will so change the landscape that my cache will forever be hidden from me as well. So be it.

Trixie felt her breath catch in her throat. Whoever wrote this was talking about buried treasure. And whoever had been reading this before she came into the room was therefore looking for buried treasure. Trixie quickly picked up the book and thumbed through the pages to see whose diary it was. As she did, the diary flopped open to a yellowed page with a picture on it. Bending down to get a better look, Trixie saw that it was a map.

"Holy cow!" Trixie whistled softly.

The crudely drawn map showed several roads, a forest, three hills, the name "Depew," and a large X next to something that looked like a cave entrance.

"This is it!" Trixie gasped. "But I can't take the book out of the archives. Oh, no. What am I going to do?"

Trixie tried to memorize the map, but it was no use. She realized she'd have to make a copy of it, but how? Desperately, she looked for a piece of paper. But there were no pads or pencils in the little room. Quickly turning the book over, she saw a name on the front: EDWARD PALMER.

Then she remembered who Edward Palmer was. She'd learned about him in history class. He was a Tory spy who'd been hung on Gallows Hill, right near Sleepyside, in 1777. Since the diary entry was dated January 3, 1777, Palmer had probably been caught and hanged some time after that. It was impossible to know if he had ever returned to the cave to get his gold. That meant the gold might still be buried—and someone besides Trixie Belden knew about it, too!

I'll just run over to the library, Trixie thought. *I'm sure the librarian will lend me some paper and a pencil. It'll only take me a minute.*

Pushing the chair back with a loud scrape, Trixie threw open the door to the archive room. She dashed up the dimly lit staircase that led to the main floor.

7 * The Stolen Clue

TRIXIE MANAGED to get to the front door without being seen by Jake Hanson. She knew that if Mr. Hanson were to see her leaving, he'd lock the door, and she'd have to waste time trying to get him to let her back inside. Since it was almost closing time, he might not let her in at all. Then the map and the diary would have to wait until tomorrow afternoon —and that might be too late.

Trixie dashed out of the building and broke into a run. After the darkness of the archive room, her eyes needed to adjust to the sunlight. As they did, she saw a yellow Volkswagen parked at the curb in front of the building. Hearing the clatter of Trixie's shoes on the pavement, the man in the car looked up. It was Harry!

Trixie gasped. What was Harry doing at the Historical Society? She'd thought that Charles was the one who was interested in the archives. Then she remembered something—both men were interested in historical materials. That was what their conversation in the woods was all about—a map! A treasure map, in all likelihood.

The afternoon sun glancing into the car window made it hard for the man inside to see her. He narrowed his eyes to a squint, then a shock of recognition flickered across his face. With a sharp scowl, Harry started the engine of the car, and swiftly drove around the corner and out of sight.

I wonder what his problem is, Trixie thought. *Why is he upset to see me? The map —maybe he knows I found the map! Oh, brother. I'd better hurry and make a copy of that map. Then I'll hide the book somewhere on the shelves.*

Trixie ran the fifty yards to the library and practically dragged Honey from her chair.

"What are you doing?" Honey gasped, her voice a whispered protest.

"Quick," Trixie panted, trying to get her breath, "do you have a pencil and a piece of paper?"

"No," Honey said. "What's the matter? Why are you pulling on me so hard?"

"You'll see in a minute, but I haven't got time to explain now. Please try to borrow a pencil and paper from the librarian. I have to get back to the archive room."

Honey quickly did as Trixie asked, but she was confused. Trixie was already at the door when Honey caught up with her.

Out on the sidewalk, Trixie started running, and Honey had to run to keep up with her.

"This had better be good," Honey gasped as the two girls went down the stairs to the archive room.

"It is," Trixie answered with a sly smile. "I just want it to be a surprise."

But what a surprise Trixie had waiting for her when she opened the door to the room. The table was bare, and the little leather-bound book was gone.

"It was right here!" Trixie cried. "I left it here not five minutes ago."

"*What* was right here, Trixie?" Honey

asked in an exasperated tone. "Now will you please tell me what's going on?"

"The diary and the map," Trixie moaned. "Wait! Maybe someone put it back on the shelves."

"What diary? What map?" Honey asked, watching Trixie race madly around the room, running her fingers across the backs of all the books.

"Edward Palmer's diary, of course," Trixie answered, slightly distracted. "And the map showing where he buried his treasure."

"Run that by me one more time, Trixie Belden," Honey said. "You found a diary and a treasure map?"

"That's exactly what I found," Trixie said, turning to face her friend. "Hey, wait a minute. That yellow pad wasn't on the chair when I was here before. Someone must have come down while I was at the library."

Suddenly there was a loud banging in the room. Trixie and Honey both jumped, startled by the unexpected noise.

"It's only the window," Trixie whispered with a sigh of relief. "The wind must have rattled it."

Sure enough, a small window located high

up on the wall was swinging loose from its top hinges. The window lock was knocking against the metal mount that secured it when it was closed.

"That window wasn't open before," Trixie said suspiciously.

Suddenly Trixie noticed that one of the chairs had been pulled over to the window. She quickly stepped up on the seat. Gripping the bottom of the window jamb with both hands, she was able to pull herself up for a better look outside.

"Look!" she gasped. "Someone's running across the lawn." Honey quickly joined her on the chair.

Sure enough, a dark-haired man was running across the back lawn, heading for the thick underbrush that surrounded the old building. Trixie could see that he was carrying something small, rectangular, and brown in his hand.

"Hey, you!" Trixie yelled. "Come back with that!"

But the man didn't stop or turn around.

"That's it!" she screeched. "I bet that was Charles! He stole the diary. Harry was parked outside when I came out. He probably told

Charles I was gone for good so he could continue working with the book. When Charles heard us coming, the only escape was out the window. That's why the chair was pulled over."

"Let's follow him," Honey said quickly.

The two girls raced up the stairs, out the door, and around to the back of the building. But the man had disappeared.

"I'm sure it was Charles Miller," Trixie said, more calmly this time. "That diary was exactly what he was after. He probably found the map when he was in the archive room this morning with Brian. But he couldn't steal it under Brian's nose, so he had to come back for it."

"Let's double-check," Honey said reasonably. "It's possible that the diary or the map is still there. Maybe that wasn't what he was carrying at all."

"Maybe you're right," Trixie said.

They went back into the building, passing Jake Hanson on the way. He smiled happily at them and nodded.

"Just let me know when you're through," he called after them. "It's almost closing time, but enjoy your history!"

Back in the room, faced with the rows and

rows of books, Trixie realized the task might be impossible. She worried that Jake Hanson had perhaps put the book away, and that she'd lose time looking for it. Then, seeing the yellow pad on the chair, Trixie had an idea. *I wonder . . .* she thought.

Using her pencil, she began to rub the side of the lead lightly across the pad. As she covered the entire page with graphite, delicate white lines began to appear. It was a handmade copy of the map!

"Look at this, Honey," Trixie said. "This is the map! Whoever was down here made a copy of it, just the way I was going to. I bet when he heard us coming back, he grabbed his copy of the map along with the book, so we wouldn't be able to make a copy of our own."

"That's it?" Honey said, looking at the faint outlines Trixie had revealed with her pencil rubbing.

"That's it!" Trixie replied proudly. "Charles didn't know I could make a rubbing of the impression a pencil makes through a sheet of paper. An old detective trick!"

"What's that word?" Honey asked as she studied the pale rubbing. "The X and the roads are clear, but those roads could be any-where."

Trixie thought hard for a moment, trying to remember.

"I've got it. The map had only one word on it—Depew. Now all we have to do is find out if that's the name of someplace around here."

"I don't think I've ever heard that name," Honey pondered. "The map may not be of this area."

"No," Trixie countered. "I think the map is of someplace nearby. That's why Charles and Harry are interested in it."

"Maybe we should go back to the library. The librarian might be able to help us."

"Good idea," Trixie said. "We'd better close and lock the window, though. It looks like it might rain."

The girls locked the little window, and moved the chair back to the table where it belonged.

"I'm going to take this pad," Trixie said as they closed the door behind them. "I need proof that I made a rubbing of the map."

"Right. And we could also use it to make notes on," Honey suggested.

Trixie and Honey slowly climbed the stairs. Jake Hanson was sitting at his desk near the entrance.

"Well, girls," he said, "did you find anything interesting?"

"Yes, sir," Trixie answered. "We certainly did. But we're finished now, so you can lock the door."

Mr. Hanson pulled himself slowly out of the chair and crossed the foyer.

"Yessiree," he said with a laugh. "It sure is nice to see such enthusiastic young people. Lotta young people are getting interested in those archives, and it's a good thing. I always have held with learning from the mistakes of history, heh-heh. Most people wait until they're too old to read history. By then, they've already made all their mistakes."

"Thanks very much, Mr. Hanson," Honey called after him.

"No problem, young lady," he replied from the stairs. "Just drop by anytime, anytime."

Trixie and Honey walked back to the library. It was cool and quiet inside, and they were grateful for the water fountain. Trixie felt hot, and she let the cool stream of water run over her wrists for a while. Honey looked as neat and comfortable as always. When they felt a little more settled, they went over to the information desk.

"I don't know," mused Mrs. Field, the librarian. "Depew . . . that name doesn't ring a bell. But I have a few books here that might help you. They're in the reserve collection, so I'm afraid you can't take them out of the library."

"That's all right, Mrs. Field," Trixie replied. "We'll work at one of the tables."

"You girls just wait here," the pleasant older woman said. "I'll be right back."

Trixie and Honey sank down onto the comfortable old wooden chairs, and stuck their feet out under the table.

Soon Mrs. Field returned with a stack of old volumes.

"Now, I don't know which of these will be most helpful," she said, putting them down on the table. "I'd try *History of the Province of New York* first. It was written by William Smith in 1757, and it might have a listing of the old families. There is also *Letters from an American Farmer* by St. John de Crèvecoeur. Oh, and this book on architecture might be helpful, because it describes various great houses of the Pre-Revolutionary period. Perhaps the family you're thinking of is mentioned there."

"Oh, thank you," Trixie said. She tried to smile cheerfully, but the sight of all those fat books with their tiny print made her feel gloomy.

"You're welcome, Trixie," the woman said. "And if you need anything else, just ask. I'll be at my desk."

"Gleeps," Trixie sighed after Mrs. Field was out of earshot. "Look at these books! It's going to take us all week to find anything."

"No, it won't," Honey said, opening one quickly. "We'll check the indexes first. If we don't find the name listed, we can just skim the pages. That's easy enough."

"Easy for you, maybe," Trixie muttered. "You're good at that sort of thing."

"Stop grousing and read," Honey replied with a laugh. "We'll have our answer in no time."

But two hours later, at closing time, the girls hadn't found anything about a family called Depew. In fact, there was no mention at all of the name. They were very discouraged.

"Now what?" Trixie muttered after they'd

handed the books back to Mrs. Field and thanked her.

"Now we go home," Honey said. "We need a rest."

"I don't feel like resting," Trixie replied sadly. "Why don't we take the horses out? It doesn't look like it will rain anymore."

"That's a great idea," Honey answered. "Regan has been after me to exercise the horses. I haven't had a minute since we started working on the dig, though."

"Maybe we can think while we ride," Trixie said as she got on her bike.

The Wheelers had a stable and several horses which the Bob-Whites were encouraged to exercise. Mrs. Wheeler's horse, Lady, was Trixie's favorite. She was a dappled gray mare who had an unusual habit of "blowing herself up" when being saddled. Usually the cinch had to be retightened after riding some distance because the saddle would start to slip. Susie was a beautiful black mare that Trixie and Honey had purchased for Miss Trask with the reward money they'd earned after solving a mystery. Although Honey had her own horse, she often rode Susie because she was so gentle.

Regan was delighted to see the girls, and he quickly saddled Susie and Lady.

"Now don't get them overheated," he warned as they rode out of the stable. "And make sure you bring them back soon, and groom them, and put away the tack. And be careful."

"We will," Honey called as she and Trixie trotted off down the driveway. Bill Regan took his job seriously. He had been known to get upset with them if they did anything careless or unsafe while riding.

"We'll see you later!" Trixie called over her shoulder. "And don't worry about us. We're always very careful."

The two girls broke into a canter and disappeared down one of the smooth trails through the woods.

8 * More Information

THE SHADED PATH that Susie and Lady followed soon emerged onto the shoulder of Glen Road. After checking for traffic in both directions, the girls guided their horses across the road and headed onto a new path. They followed it for a while, and then picked up another of the many paths that threaded through the preserve. This one led past the dig site, but the girls didn't mind.

"It's late," Trixie said, "and Charles has probably left for the city by now. Why don't we swing past the village site and see if we can find anything there that looks like what was on the map."

Soon the horses broke through into the bug-infested part of the woods where the village site was located. No one was there, and Trixie slowly slid off Lady and started walking around. Suddenly she stopped.

The little clearing sloped gradually up a slight rise. Trixie was standing near a large fallen tree. A few feet in front of her, a huge hole had been dug out of the hummock, and piles of fresh dirt were scattered all around the hole.

"Wow," Honey said with a whistle as she came up behind Trixie to survey the rubble. "Somebody was pretty busy here this afternoon."

"He certainly was," Trixie agreed. "And it doesn't look as if he was using proper archaeological methods, either."

"Whoever did this used a shovel and a pick," Honey agreed. "It would take a year to get this much dirt out using that little scratching tool Professor Conroy gave us."

"No kidding," Trixie said. "No sifting or anything! You can bet that whoever dug this hole wasn't looking for any Indian artifacts. He was looking for something else!"

"Unless, of course, he wasn't an archaeologist," Honey said with a wry smile.

"Oh, I think an archaeologist dug this hole," Trixie muttered. "And there's only one archaeologist I can think of who would bother."

"Right. The archaeologist who thinks he found a treasure map in the Historical Society archive room!"

"He may have the treasure map," Trixie said, grinning, "but by the looks of this hole, I don't think he found the treasure yet. Do you?"

"Nope."

"This is probably the wrong place," Trixie said with a laugh as she got back on her horse. "Well, I hope he enjoys digging holes."

Honey laughed too. "And it looks like he's got an awful lot of digging ahead of him!"

They rode away from the village site. The day had cooled down, so they decided to keep the horses out for a while longer before returning to the stables. They chose a path through a blackberry thicket. Stopping briefly, they pulled some ripe berries off the bushes and popped them into their mouths. Trixie decided they should return in a few days and pick the rest before the birds got to them. She knew her mother would use them to make her special blackberry jam.

They rode on until they reached the edge of Mrs. Vanderpoel's property, then they turned back. Going past the old orchard, Trixie pulled up her horse. There in the orchard was Old Brom. A chubby old man with a bush of white whiskers, he lived in a small cottage on the land which had belonged to his family since the seventeenth century. Now the land was part of the Wheeler game preserve. Very proud, and usually very shy, Old Brom was a treasure trove of wonderful old ghost stories which he liked to tell to the neighborhood children.

"Let's ask Brom if he knows the name 'Depew,'" Trixie suggested. "After all, he knows so much about this area."

The girls dismounted, looped the bridles around a fence post, and walked over to Old Brom.

"Nice day," he mumbled into his long beard. "Care for an apple?"

"No thanks, Brom," Trixie said. "We were wondering about something, and thought maybe you could help us."

"Dunno," Brom replied tersely. Then his eyes twinkled. "Mebbe."

"Have you ever heard of the name 'Depew' in these parts?" Honey asked. "We think maybe it was an old family that died out."

"Depew," Brom said slowly. "Of course, I've heard of the Depews. Long time ago, though. All history now."

"Really?" Trixie gasped. "Where was their property?"

"Right here," Brom said with a shy smile. "Well, not here, exactly. Back down Glen Road a ways. Right across from the Wheeler place. Used to be a big old mansion, but it burned down in a mysterious fire long about the time of the Revolution. Never did get built back up again.

"Owned all the land around here, the Depews did. Some say the son went crazy after the place burned down. I don't know that for sure, of course, but he never did come back. Disappeared. Land was later bought by the family that built your place, Honey."

Trixie shot Honey a warning look.

"That's really interesting, Brom," Honey said slowly. She realized that it was probably best not to mention why they wanted to know about the Depews.

"Glad to oblige," Brom said. "As a matter of fact, there's a good ghost story about the Depews, but I'll tell you the next time I see you. Have to get over to see Mrs. Vanderpoel. Promised her I'd bring her some apples. She's going to bake a pie."

"And give it to you to eat, right?" Trixie asked merrily. "She makes the best pies in the world."

"That she does," Brom answered. "I'd pick apples for Mrs. V. any day, as long as I get to eat some of her pie."

"Thanks for your help," Trixie said. "We have to get back, too. Regan gets upset if we keep the horses out too long."

Trixie and Honey waved good-bye to Brom and quickly trotted the horses along the path to Glen Road. They knew it would be quicker going back on the road than through the paths, and it was getting dark.

"What a break," Trixie said. "The Depew house was right here on the preserve. I'll bet the cave is right where Charles thinks it is!"

"Me, too," said Honey. "We'd better look at that map more closely. If Charles is on the right track, so are we."

"I'd be a lot more comfortable if *all* the Bob-Whites could investigate this one," Trixie stated. "Let's call a short meeting for tonight after dinner."

That night at the clubhouse, Trixie explained what had happened to the assembled Bob-Whites. Di and Dan sat on the floor, while Mart paced back and forth eating crackers out of a giant economy-sized box. Reddy was there, too, watching Mart pace the way a judge watches a tennis match. Back and forth, back and forth went Reddy's head. Brian looked bored.

"After Charles took the diary, I made a rubbing of what had been drawn on the pad," Trixie said. "I have a copy of the map right here. The only problem was finding out where the Depew property was. Luckily, we ran into Old Brom, and he told us that the whole game preserve was once owned by the Depew family. Their house was across the road from the Manor House, so that puts it right where the dig site is now."

"Ved-dy in-ter-est-ing, Miss Belden," Mart mumbled through a mouthful of crackers. "Do you have these insights often?"

Trixie ignored Mart's remark and went right on talking. "My theory is that Charles

Miller somehow found out that there was treasure on this land, and he decided to dig for it. But Professor Conroy disrupted his plans, first by appointing him student head of the dig, and then by assigning us to the very spot where Charles thought the treasure was buried. Charles hit Professor Conroy on the head to get him out of the way for a while—just long enough for him to find the treasure. The trouble was, Honey and I got in his way. First we showed up on the village site; and then we found the diary that he left on the table in the archive room."

"I think we should all investigate the village site before Charles gets back from the city tomorrow morning," Honey said. "We know he's already started digging for the treasure, because we saw a giant hole there this afternoon when we rode by on our horses."

"Show me the alleged map," Mart said. "This theory isn't very convincing so far."

Trixie reached into the pocket of her shorts and pulled out the rubbing she'd made earlier, along with another piece of paper.

"I recopied it so it would be easier to read," she said as she handed both pieces of paper to her skeptical brother.

Mart examined the map, then said with a shrug, "Well, why not? Going on a treasure hunt is always fun. And we can always catch fireflies if we don't find any treasure."

"Well, I'm not going to get involved in this nonsense," Brian said moodily. "I don't believe all this stuff about a treasure, and what's more, I think you're all wrong about Charles."

Trixie felt bad that Brian wasn't taking her seriously, but she had to continue her investigation, anyway. "I'm sorry. I'd like your help," she said to her brother. "But I know you need more proof, and I'll find it sooner or later."

Brian went over to the door. "I'm sorry too, Trix. But this is one mystery I'm not interested in. Count me out."

The door closed behind him.

There was a short silence after Brian left. Then Dan asked, "Do we have any flashlights here? There's no point in all of us staggering around in the woods, bumping into each other."

"Here are two," Di said. "That means we need three more."

"I'll run up to the garage and get them," Honey said, heading for the door. "I know where they're kept."

Honey returned a few moments later, and the five young people were ready to go investigating.

"This is exciting," Mart said. "All we have to do is find a treasure before we're eaten alive by mosquitoes."

Walking quickly, the Bob-Whites reached the village site through one of the back paths. They didn't want to alert the graduate students to their presence. Reddy was crashing around in and out of the bushes, making a lot of noise. Trixie tried to hush him up and make the excited dog walk quietly beside her, but it was no use. Reddy was intoxicated by the scent of small animals and was not about to be controlled. Sounds of noisy laughter and singing floated through the trees. It was obvious that even if the interlopers were to set off a few firecrackers, the students wouldn't have the slightest inkling that they weren't alone.

Once at the village site, Trixie started digging away with her hands at the low hillside where Charles had begun his search. Great clods of dirt went flying behind her. Dan found a long stick and was poking the earth to see if it sank in anywhere. Mart was marching back and forth giving unwanted advice.

"Mart, if you're so smart," Trixie finally said, looking up from her digging, "why didn't you remember to bring a shovel? It's not easy to dig for treasure with your bare hands."

"Clever," Mart said, scratching his chin. "Very clever—for a novice."

"Novice indeed!" Trixie said with a snort.

Reddy, inspired by Trixie's digging, started digging his own hole right next to her. In seconds, a thick spray of dirt coated Trixie from head to toe.

"Stop that, Reddy!" she scolded.

Reddy jumped up and down, covering Trixie with dog kisses, and then went happily back to his digging.

"Get the dog to do the dirty work," Mart said with a smirk.

In the meantime, Dan and Di were examining the map with their flashlights.

"If there were a cave around here, it would have to be made of limestone," Dan said thoughtfully. "But there are no rock formations anywhere in this area, so the cave would have to be underground, not in the side of a hill. I think Charles was digging in the wrong place."

"Isn't that a tree?" Di said, pointing to a spot

on the map. "I guess it would have to be a pretty big tree by now, since that map was drawn at least two hundred years ago."

"Wait a minute," Trixie said. "Maybe this giant log is part of that old tree. It certainly looks fat enough to be over two hundred years old. And the other trees around here look like second growth. They're not tall, and their trunks are thin. Maybe this place was once a meadow."

"All this conjecture is ridiculous without a shovel," Mart said pompously. "I'm glad I thought of it."

"You didn't think of it," Trixie muttered.

Honey quickly jabbed her elbow into Trixie's ribs.

"Yes, he did," Honey said quickly. "And since he thought of it, he should be the one to go get it."

"Great thinking, Honey," Trixie put in with a laugh. "Bring two while you're at it—they're small."

"I'd better go with you," Dan said. "We wouldn't want you to get lost in the woods."

"I would *never* get lost in the woods, old man," Mart was saying as they left the clearing. "But I'm glad you came along. I need someone to carry the shovels for me."

The girls heard Dan burst out laughing. "That's why I brought *you,* Mart," he joked.

Reddy bounded through the bushes after the two boys.

"There goes our digging machine," said Trixie. "Let's just sit down and wait for the shovels."

Honey laughed and tossed her hair. "You're right," she said. "There's no sense breaking a fingernail over something as minor as a treasure."

"Fingernail?" Di said glumly. "We'd more likely break an ankle trying to see our way in the dark. Sitting down is not only restful, it's smart, if you ask me."

The three girls sat down to wait.

9 * The Ghost

TRIXIE, HONEY, AND DI sat huddled together on the fallen log, and listened. The sounds made by Mart and Dan stomping through the woods grew faint. Soon all was silent, and Trixie felt a shiver of apprehension between her shoulder blades.

"It sure is dark in these woods," Honey said miserably.

"It's not so dark," Trixie answered, trying to sound cheerful. Then she looked around. The sun was sinking rapidly. "Well, maybe it's a *little* dark," she added.

111

"I don't like being in the woods in the dark," Di said. "I should have stayed home."

"What makes you say a thing like that?" Trixie asked loudly. She hoped the sound of her own words would make everyone feel better—herself included. "This is going to be exciting. The boys will be back any minute now, and then we'll have a real treasure hunt!"

But Trixie's voice had a false ring. The cheerful tones sounded hollow.

After a few moments, as if on cue, the three friends moved closer together on the log. Soon their shoulders were touching.

"D-do you think there are g-ghosts in these woods?" Di stammered.

"Don't be silly," Honey snapped. "There's no such thing as a ghost."

Di wasn't convinced. "How can you be so sure?"

"Honey's right," Trixie said meekly. "There aren't any ghosts."

"Then why are you looking all around like that?" Di asked Trixie.

Trixie didn't have an answer to Di's question. None of the girls could think of anything else to say. Di started to whistle. Honey began to hum. The bugs droned on, and the cicadas seemed louder than usual. Suddenly the girls became aware of another noise, which was rapidly getting louder than the insects.

Trixie snapped her head around just in time to see a weird, glowing apparition float through the trees and swoop to the edge of the clearing. Before she could open her mouth, the horrible thing began to wail. Its voice was a high-pitched, eerie quaver.

The three girls grabbed each other as the skeletal figure, draped in moldy-looking rags and tendrils of cobwebs and tree roots, came closer and closer. Its head looked like an old skull, with long gray hair that fell down over empty eye sockets. An iridescent yellow glow emanated from its body as it menacingly waved a big gnarled stick in their direction.

"A ghost!" Di shrieked. Her voice was a thin wail, almost as high-pitched as the horrible noise coming from the ugly creature.

Then, just as suddenly as it had appeared, the glowing thing floated off into the trees. Trixie dropped her flashlight. It landed on the log with a loud thump. She groped blindly until she finally found the reassuring cylindrical object. Grasping it hard, she started to stand up. Honey and Di rose at the same time.

With a speed born of fear, the three girls launched themselves off the log and down the path that led out of the clearing, far away from the awful monster. They raced toward the clubhouse.

"I told you," Trixie gasped as they crossed Glen Road. "The ghosts of those dead Indians are angry at us! We've been tramping all over their sacred burial ground."

At last the girls reached the clubhouse. Di moaned softly as they slumped against the side of the building. "I'm sorry I ever got mixed up in this."

"It *couldn't* have been a ghost," Honey said, panting heavily. "I don't believe in them, and neither should you. There has to be another explanation, there just has to."

Trixie's breathing was returning to normal, and with it, her ability to think clearly. "I wonder . . ." she began. "Remember the headless horseman, Honey?"

"Do I ever," Honey replied.

"That time, someone dressed up as a ghostly horseman to scare us away from a mystery. I'll bet that silly ghost was doing the same thing. But who was it?"

"I don't c-care," Di said, her voice quavering. "I'm scared. What happened to Mart and Dan, anyway? Why aren't they here?"

Lost in trying to figure out who the ghost could have been, Trixie had forgotten all about the boys. But now, shaking herself out of her musing, she became aware of a commotion coming from the direction of the Manor House.

"I wonder what's happening at the Manor House?" Trixie asked. Without waiting for an answer, she started running up the driveway. Honey and Di followed right behind her. As they rounded the bend, they saw lights blazing. The big front door was wide open, spilling light onto the veranda and the circular drive. People were moving about inside, and the girls could hear the faint whine of a police siren heading their way.

"What the . . ." Trixie began. But before she could voice the question, Mart came bounding down the steps to meet them.

"You girls missed everything," he said. "Out in the woods chasing phony treasure, while we were here with the real action!"

"What happened?" Honey asked, her voice heavy with dread. She started for the house. "I'd better see if Miss Trask is all right."

The three young people quickly followed Honey into the house. There was Miss Trask, standing in the middle of a pile of silver and haphazardly scattered paintings.

"Honey," she said with a weak smile. "Thank heavens you're here!"

"What happened?" Honey asked softly as her eyes took in the mess in the foyer. "Why is all this stuff here on the floor?"

"Someone tried to rob the house," Miss Trask said, sounding shaken. "I was upstairs in my room, reading, and the house was dark. I guess they thought no one was home. I heard footsteps downstairs and I thought it was you, so I opened my door and called you—just to let you know I was awake.

"Suddenly there was all this thumping, then the sound of a car starting. I started to go downstairs, because I thought that you might be in some kind of trouble. But when I flipped on the light switch, there was no one here, just this pile of things. I started to scream and then I heard the sound of crunching metal, as if a car had hit something."

"I know," said Regan. He was wearing his pajamas, and had just come out of the dining room. "That's when I woke up. I heard the crash and I heard Miss Trask screaming, so I ran up to the house. It looks as if she interrupted the burglars. They left before loading up all these valuables."

"That's when we came in," Dan said, looking around grimly. "We were just coming out of the woods when a car shot out of the driveway."

"It was probably the getaway car," Mart said helpfully.

"I do hope nothing's missing," said Miss Trask. Her voice sounded worried and frightened as she gestured to the glittering array in the hall. "But I just can't go through it all now. There's so much."

"Here come the police," Bill Regan said. "That sure was quick!"

The sirens came screaming up the driveway, then the noise was abruptly cut off. The sound of car doors slamming was followed by heavy footsteps as Sergeant Molinson and two other policemen came striding into the house.

"It looks like you stopped them before too much was taken," Sergeant Molinson said, looking around. "Have you touched anything?"

"No, sergeant," Regan answered quietly. "This is exactly the way we found it."

Miss Trask had been looking suspiciously at the pile, when suddenly a smile of relief crossed her face. "Well, at least the Renoir wasn't in the group of paintings they planned to take," she said. "Maybe they didn't see it. It is rather small, you know."

"And who was in the house at the time?" asked the sergeant, glancing briefly at the crowd of young people in the room.

"Only me," said Miss Trask. "Regan and the boys heard me screaming, and they came first. Then Trixie, Honey, and Di arrived after we'd called you. Mart and Dan may have seen the car, however."

Sergeant Molinson shifted his attention to the two boys. "Is what Miss Trask says correct? Did you see the car?"

"Well, yes and no," Mart said sheepishly. "We saw a car come out of the driveway at top speed, but we couldn't see what kind of car it was. It was too dark."

"They were driving without headlights, sir," Dan said.

Sergeant Molinson grunted. Then he turned to his men. "I'll bet it's the same bunch. Take a look around, will you?"

The two policemen left the room, one heading into the living room, and the other out the front door.

"The men will see if they can find any clues around the house," he said glumly. "We'll dust for fingerprints, of course. But if it's the same burglars, they won't leave any prints. Now, Miss Trask, would you step into the living room with me? I'd like to ask you a few questions."

Miss Trask led the way. When the sergeant got to the large double doors, he turned back to the little group in the foyer. "Please don't leave yet," he told them. "I'd like to talk with you when I'm through."

Honey sank down on a damask chair and began to rub her forehead. "I can't believe it," she said weakly. "I'd better call my parents. They have to know about this."

Di sat down on the arm of the chair and rubbed the back of Honey's neck. Trixie was lost in thought again. Gripping her flashlight, she turned and walked out the front door.

"Hey, Trixie," Mart called after her, "Sergeant Molinson said—"

"I know what he said, and I'm coming right back," Trixie said hastily. "There's something I have to check first. It might be a clue."

Trixie quickly walked down the broad front steps of the Manor House, and stood uncertainly in the driveway. Turning on the flashlight, she scanned the loose gravel. The broad beam of light swung slowly back and forth as she walked around the circular drive. At last, on the east side of the great curve, she found what she was looking for—deep skid marks in the gravel.

Thoughtfully, she stared at the marks, determining their direction. Then Trixie continued along the circular drive until she came to the point where it joined the tree-lined road leading off the estate. There at the corner of the well-manicured lawn stood a big oak tree. Trixie walked over to it and shone her flashlight beam on the lower part of its trunk.

What she saw confirmed her suspicions. Hunks of bark had been gouged out of the tree. *This must have been what the car hit,* Trixie reasoned. *Miss Trask said she'd heard the sound of crunching metal after the car had started. If the burglars were driving fast without headlights, they probably missed the turn right here.* Bending close, Trixie carefully scanned the damaged tree and found flakes of yellow paint stuck to the trunk.

"Just as I thought," she muttered.

Straightening up quickly, Trixie ran back to the house and went inside. Mart and Dan were with Sergeant Molinson, and Honey was on the phone, speaking tearfully with her father. Miss Trask stood next to her, an arm resting affectionately on the girl's shoulders.

Not wanting to interrupt, Trixie went over to Di, who was looking nervously at the pile of almost-stolen goods.

"Why is Honey crying?" Trixie asked softly.

"It's the Renoir," Di whispered back. "When Miss Trask was in the living room with Sergeant Molinson, she saw that it wasn't hanging on the wall. Since it isn't in the pile, either, it must be gone."

"Oh, no," Trixie said. "What are they going to do?"

"Try to catch the burglars, I guess," Di answered sadly. "But if the newspaper stories are true, that won't be easy. Sergeant Molinson thinks it's the same bunch, and they haven't been able to catch them so far."

The double doors to the living room swung open, and a subdued Dan and Mart came out into the foyer.

"Sorry we couldn't be of more help," Dan said.

"Don't worry about it," Sergeant Molinson said gruffly. "I think that's all for now. You kids better get home."

"What about us?" Trixie asked. "Don't you need to question us, too? I think I might have a clue."

"I doubt it, since you weren't here when all this happened," Sergeant Molinson answered abruptly. He turned to Dan and Mart. "Would you see that the young ladies get home safely? We have a lot more work ahead of us, and it's past their bedtime."

"Past my bedtime!" Trixie burst out angrily. But at a warning glance from Dan, she quieted down, a look of grim determination on her face.

If the sergeant isn't interested in what I have to say, she thought, *then I can't force him to listen.*

"It would be better for all concerned if you kids didn't get involved," the sergeant said with a pointed stare at Trixie. He never liked it when Trixie tried to get involved in a case. "Now I want you all to head on home."

Everyone said their good-byes. Dan and Mart accompanied Di and Trixie down the driveway. When they reached Glen Road, they separated. Dan walked Di home since it was on his way. The Beldens walked up the road to Crabapple Farm in silence. It had been an exciting day, and Trixie was too tired to talk. Besides, she needed to think.

"Is that you, children?" Mrs. Belden called from her bedroom.

"Yes, Moms," Trixie answered. Then she switched off the downstairs hall light and climbed slowly up the stairs. Mrs. Belden always kept the light on when the children were out late.

As she closed her bedroom door behind her, Trixie tried to organize the events of the night in a logical way. She realized with a start that in all the excitement of the burglary, she had completely forgotten to mention the ghost to anyone. She was glad that Honey and Di had seen it, too, so she couldn't be accused of making things up. But who could it have been? Who would want to go to the trouble of putting on such a creepy charade to scare them away?

Trixie considered the possible suspects. There was Charles Miller, of course. He was trying awfully hard to get her and Honey away from the village site. But Charles Miller hadn't been in Sleepyside tonight. He was working in the city, as usual.

It could have been Harry, too. But Harry drove a yellow Volkswagen, and that gave Trixie the idea that he was busy doing something else tonight—something far more lucrative than scaring a bunch of girls in the woods!

It was confusing. If Trixie's figuring was correct, both men would have to have been in two places at the same time. And that was impossible.

Trixie decided to sleep on it, and hoped that some answers would come to her by morning. As her head hit the pillow, she fell into a deep, dreamless sleep.

10 * In the Cave

AT BREAKFAST the next morning, Trixie was greeted by a very worried Helen Belden.

"Good morning, Moms," she said with a puzzled look at her mother.

"Oh, Trixie, I'm so upset. Have you seen Reddy?" Mrs. Belden's forehead was furrowed with concern. "He wasn't in the house this morning, and he isn't outside, either. Did he come home with you last night?"

Trixie's hand flew up to her mouth in horror. "Oh, no!" she gasped. "He was with us in the woods, but he went off with Mart and Dan when they went for the shovels. I didn't see him after that. I forgot—I mean, what with the burglary and everything!"

"The burglary!" Now it was Mrs. Belden's turn to look shocked. "What burglary?"

While Trixie ate her cereal, she told her mother what had happened at the Manor House the night before.

"So, you see," she finished lamely, "I wasn't even thinking about Reddy. I guess I just assumed that he came home while we were talking to Sergeant Molinson."

"This is dreadful," said Mrs. Belden. "I hope they catch the crooks. But I'm worried about Reddy. It's very unusual for him to stay out all night like this."

"Should I start looking for him right now?" Trixie asked. "I could miss work today."

"Oh no, dear," Mrs. Belden said as she cleared the table distractedly. "I would be happier if you went to work. I'll look for him this morning. I'm sure he'll turn up someplace. I just don't want to upset Bobby. You know how he gets."

"If he isn't home by this afternoon," Trixie said, "I'll look for him instead of going to the dig."

"Darling, it's 7:30," Mrs. Belden said. "I think you'd better get going. I'll make a few calls before Bobby gets up. Maybe a neighbor has seen Reddy."

Trixie grabbed her cap, and headed for the door. "See you later, Moms," she called as the door banged behind her.

Trixie was very busy all morning at the hospital. She was so worried about Reddy that she called home on her break. But no one answered the phone. It was close to 12 o'clock before she had a chance to look in on Professor Conroy.

Trixie opened the stairwell door to the second floor, and started down the corridor. But she stopped short when she saw Professor Conroy's door open, and Harry step into the hall! He glanced briefly in Trixie's direction, then disappeared around the corner, heading for the elevators.

Trixie's breath caught in her throat. Then she relaxed. *I guess he didn't recognize me in this candy-striper uniform,* she thought. *I wonder what he's doing here, and why he's visiting Professor Conroy?*

Then Trixie had a horrible thought—Harry was Charles Miller's friend, not Professor Conroy's. And it was Charles, she suspected, who had put Professor Conroy in the hospital in the first place! That might mean Harry was going to harm the professor, too.

Trixie broke into a run. She flung open the door to the professor's room.

"Oh, hello there, Miss Belden," the professor said when he saw Trixie come running in. "My, my, you certainly do rush around."

Relieved to see that the professor was all right, Trixie suddenly felt silly for the way she'd come barging in. She started to apologize. "I-I'm so sorry, Professor Conroy," she stammered. "I hope I didn't alarm you."

"Oh, no. Don't give it a second thought," he replied, smiling cheerfully. "It can get very dull just lying in bed all day without talking to anyone."

Trixie moved closer to the bed. She could see that Professor Conroy seemed to be in good spirits, yet he looked much sicker than he had the day before. There were deep, dark circles under his eyes, and his skin looked pale and gray.

"I just saw someone come out of your room," Trixie said, filled with concern. "Are you well enough to have visitors?"

Professor Conroy glanced at her sharply. "I

had no visitors," he said. "You must be mistaken."

"Why, I could have sworn I saw Harry coming out of—" Trixie began, but she stopped when she saw a look of irritation sweep over Professor Conroy's face.

"Miss Belden," he said, "perhaps whoever you *think* you saw was coming out of some other room."

Embarrassed, Trixie looked down at her feet. *I know what I saw,* she thought. *After all, there's only a vacant room and a supply closet at this end of the hall. What would Harry be doing in the supply closet?*

Her eyes came to rest on a pair of shoes neatly placed at the side of the bed. They were caked with thick, sticky mud. *The professor shouldn't be wearing shoes here. He should have some slippers,* she thought. Then Trixie remembered that the professor had come to the hospital unexpectedly. *Perhaps he doesn't have slippers, and no one thought to bring him any, either.*

"Why, you don't have any slippers," Trixie said in a rush of concern. "Would you like me to bring you a pair? They'll be more comfortable than these shoes."

Professor Conroy chuckled. "Very kind of

you to think of it, but I don't need slippers, or even shoes, for that matter. The good doctor has told me I can't get up at all, not even to use the facilities. Most distressing."

"Oh. Would you like me to put these away for you, then?"

"If you please. Most kind of you, most kind."

Thinking that sometime she would clean the mud off the professor's shoes, Trixie put them in the closet. Then she fluffed up the sick man's pillows.

Before leaving the room, Trixie said, "Feel free to ask me for anything you need, Professor Conroy. I'd be glad to help you anytime." Then she backed out the door.

"Most kind," the professor muttered drowsily. He closed his eyes and turned his head away from her.

"The poor professor," Trixie said to Honey that afternoon as they made their way to the dig site. "He looks even worse today than he did yesterday."

"I guess he took quite a knock on the head," Honey answered.

"Maybe Charles hit him harder than he'd intended," Trixie said grimly. "And that reminds me, Reddy didn't come home last night. If Moms hasn't found him yet, we should look for him in the woods, or ask the students if they've seen him."

"Reddy's probably at the dig right now," Honey said, trying to sound reassuring. "Remember, they have cookouts over the fire. He was probably lured by the smell of hot dogs and hamburgers."

"I hope you're right," Trixie said with a sigh. "Moms is really worried about him."

"I'm worried, too," Honey said. "It was nice of your mom to make us this picnic lunch, anyway."

"Well, she wanted us to start looking for Reddy right away," Trixie said. "She thought we'd waste time if we ate at home first."

Trixie and Honey trudged along the road. When they came to the main dig site, they saw a truck parked near the tents. Charles Miller and a short, heavyset man were having a loud conversation. Several graduate students were standing around listening with interest. As the girls got closer, they were able to hear better.

"I don't give a hoot what your piece of paper says," Charles was snarling at the man. "I have a copy of our order here, and it says,

'Five dozen cartons of three-by-five cards, ten boxes of large manila envelopes, two cartons of self-adhesive labels, and a gross of flat, corrugated cartons.' I won't accept this delivery, and that's final!"

"Look, buddy," the man replied sullenly, "all this slip says is to deliver a hundred cases of printed envelopes to Professor Conroy at the Wheeler game preserve, and that's what I'm gonna do. Take it or leave it."

"I'm leaving it," Charles snapped. "I refuse to sign for this delivery, and furthermore, I'm going right down to the U.P.S. office and clear up this whole mess with your supervisor."

With that, Charles stalked off the dig site. The delivery man got back into his truck, and drove off in a cloud of dust. Charles jumped into Professor Conroy's jeep and followed right behind him.

"That takes care of Charles Miller for the afternoon," Trixie said with a satisfied smile. "Let's go back to the village site and see if we can find out any more about who was digging that hole and why. We were interrupted last night, but I doubt if we'll be interrupted this afternoon."

The two girls rushed down the little path

through the woods. Halfway to the clearing, Trixie stopped short.

"Look!" she gasped, pointing her finger through the undergrowth.

Harry's yellow Volkswagen was parked in the woods, just off the path. The left front fender was dented, and a large area had lost its paint.

"See," Trixie said, "that looks like a brand-new scratch, too. It isn't rusted."

"What do you mean, 'see'?" Honey asked. "You know, sometimes you talk in riddles, Trixie Belden."

Trixie was about to answer when she heard muffled barking coming from a short distance away.

"Reddy!" she shouted, and she broke into a run.

There was no Reddy in the clearing. But oddly, the muffled barking was now even louder.

"Where *is* that silly dog," Trixie muttered as she prowled around the edge of the clearing. "I can hear him, but I haven't the slightest idea where he is."

Following the sound of his barks, Trixie went a short distance farther. Suddenly her foot slipped. Before she could grab hold of anything, she found herself shooting down a muddy incline at the base of a fat old tree stump.

She hit bottom with a spine-jarring thud. Luckily, the camper's flashlight she had hooked to her belt didn't break. The next thing she knew, a delirious Reddy was jumping all over her. She hugged the dog gratefully and took a look around. It was pitch black except for a jagged circle of light above her head.

She was in a cave!

"Trixie!" Honey's worried voice filtered through the blackness that surrounded her.

"Over here!" Trixie called out. But before she had a chance to yell, "Be careful!" Honey came sliding down into the cave with her.

Reddy was delighted to have so much company, but the girls were miserable.

"There has to be a way out of here," Trixie moaned. Great clumps of dirt landed on her head as she tried to scale the slippery side of the cave. She lost her footing again and again. "Maybe if you give me a boost, I could reach the edge."

But try as they might, they couldn't get out.

Trixie and Honey were stuck.

"Maybe we should yell," Honey suggested. "One of the students might hear us and pull us out."

"Good thinking," Trixie said. "Let's yell together. One, two, three . . ."

"Hel-l-l-lp! Hel-l-l-lp!"

Moments later, the girls were exhausted, and they gave up. It was obvious that they were too far from the main dig site for their voices to carry. The cave was damp and cold. It smelled of old mushrooms and rotting vegetation. Trixie didn't like it one bit. Finally, the two sat down and leaned back against the wall.

Trixie closed her eyes and sighed. It was getting late. Only a small shaft of light came through the hole above them. When night came, it would be darker than pitch. Trixie knew she couldn't leave her flashlight on for long—the batteries would give out. "Maybe we should try and rest," she said to Honey.

But her rest didn't last long. It was interrupted by a rustling sound nearby.

Trixie leapt to her feet. It was Reddy. His nose was buried in the paper-bag lunch that Mrs. Belden had packed for them.

"Of course!" Trixie said, patting the dog's

head. "You poor thing. You haven't eaten since yesterday."

"See, Trixie," Honey said with a laugh. "With your usual presence of mind, you held onto the picnic lunch while you were falling into the cave. At least we won't starve to death now."

"I feel just like Alice in Wonderland," Trixie said as she fed Reddy a bologna sandwich. "Remember the part where she fell down the hole?"

Honey giggled. "Maybe the White Rabbit will come and get us out."

"Better the White Rabbit than that awful Charles Miller," Trixie said. But she didn't feel like laughing.

"Charles Miller is the only person who ever comes to this part of the woods," Honey said thoughtfully. "He might be our only hope."

"That's what I'm afraid of," Trixie answered gloomily. "What if he finds us, but refuses to help us get out?"

Trixie knew that Charles Miller was looking for a cave. And it was beginning to look as if Trixie and Honey had found the very cave Charles was looking for. If he had resorted to knocking Professor Conroy over the head to get him out of the way, what would he do to keep Trixie and Honey from getting his treasure? Trixie shuddered. Absolutely no one knew where they were. She hoped Charles Miller wouldn't figure that out. They might never get out of this cave alive!

11 * Trapped!

TRIXIE HAD no idea how long they'd been sitting in the cave, but she could see from the angle of the sun glancing in through the opening that it was probably late afternoon.

"This is ridiculous," Trixie said finally. "I'm going to explore this cave. There has to be another way out."

"Oh, Trixie," Honey said, sounding frightened, "please be careful. All I can think of is those stories I've heard about people who get lost exploring in underground caves. Wouldn't you rather sit here and wait for someone to come and rescue us?"

"No, I wouldn't," Trixie replied firmly. "And I promise I'll be careful, so please don't worry."

"Do you think I should go with you?"

"No. You stay right there. Besides, I might not be going anywhere," Trixie said with a laugh. She stood up and switched on her flashlight. Shining it along the edges of the cave walls, she began to examine the grim place with great care. Trixie judged that the cave was about nine feet deep, and not large. It was like a small subterranean room. Unfortunately, the walls were fairly straight and smooth, with no rock outcroppings to get a foothold on. Tree roots had broken through in places and they hung down eerily, like long, grasping fingers reaching out.

Upon closer examination, Trixie noticed that the walls were made of dirt, not rock. She had always thought that caves had rocky walls, but this one seemed to have slimy, mud walls. *Ugh,* she thought. *No wonder they had been so impossible to climb.*

There didn't seem to be any openings other

than the one in the roof. But all the hanging roots made Trixie think there might be an opening hidden behind the tangled growth. *I hope there are no bats, or rats, or anything else in here,* she thought with a shudder.

She moved closer to one side of the cave where a gnarled, wet-looking spray of roots stuck through the wall. Reaching up to pull aside some of the finer branches, Trixie jumped in alarm as a small bug skittered across her hand. She held back a scream, not wanting to upset Honey. But there was no opening hidden by the roots; just a slimy, blank wall of mud and dirt. She checked each root clump, but found the same thing each time.

As Trixie explored the small cave, she began to notice something unusual about it. Carefully, she retraced her steps just to make sure that she wasn't jumping to any incorrect conclusions. Finally she couldn't keep quiet any longer.

"This place has a funny shape for a cave," she said to Honey. "It looks almost square. I doubt that Mother Nature would make a square cave."

"I don't understand what you mean," Honey said.

"Let me see . . ." Trixie muttered to herself. "I wonder if . . ."

Picking up a loose rock, Trixie began to scrape away at the dirt on one of the walls.

After a few good long pulls, she began to scrape harder and faster. It was just as she'd suspected.

"Hey! This isn't a cave at all," Trixie exclaimed. "It's an old cellar!"

"A cellar?" Honey said with a gasp.

"Look at this," Trixie said, shining the flashlight where she'd been scraping. "These are evenly laid stones. This is an old foundation!"

Honey leapt to her feet. Sure enough, just as Trixie had said, the wall was made of perfectly fitted square blocks. The stones looked like hewn granite.

Before Trixie or Honey could think about their next move, they heard a noise outside. It was the sound of a shovel striking stone.

Trixie quickly put her finger to her lips. Reddy, happily full of bologna sandwiches, was sleeping peacefully in the corner.

"I'm pretty sure it's Charles Miller," Trixie whispered. "Keep quiet. Maybe he won't find us."

"Why should we be quiet?" Honey whispered back, perplexed. "Why can't we yell, so he can save us?"

"Because he may *not* save us, that's why," Trixie hissed. "He's the one who hits people on the head for interfering with his silly treasure hunt! What do you think he's going to do to us once he finds out we're still snooping around here?"

"I don't care!" Honey wailed. "I don't like it down here—it's cold and creepy. I want to go home. I'm going to yell for help."

"Okay, okay," Trixie said forlornly. "We might as well start yelling. But I still don't feel right about it."

They both began to shout as loudly as they could. Reddy immediately woke up and started barking, too. Suddenly the shovel noise stopped, and they could hear twigs snapping as Charles started looking for the place the voices were coming from. He seemed to be having a hard time of it.

"Over here!" Trixie yelled. "But be careful! We're down a hole, and we can't get out!"

A few moments later, Charles Miller stuck his head through the opening and looked at them in great surprise.

"What are you doing down there?" he asked, incredulous.

"We're stuck, silly," Trixie said, getting very annoyed. "If we could get out, then we'd be out, wouldn't we?"

"Please help us," Honey pleaded. "Do you have a rope or something? It's awful down here."

For a moment Charles was silent. A number of conflicting emotions seemed to flicker across his face—surprise, anger, fear. It was the expression of fear that worried Trixie the most. If Charles Miller really did have something to hide, all her worst thoughts would prove correct. Then he spoke.

"I don't know," he said slowly. "Maybe I will and maybe I won't."

"You *have* to help us," Honey wailed.

"Maybe," Charles said with a nasty smile. "But I have to do something first."

"What do you mean, 'do something'?" Trixie shouted.

Charles pulled his head out of the opening. "Don't go away now!" he said with a grim laugh.

"I told you," Trixie muttered. "Let's find a stick or a big rock. We should at least try and protect ourselves."

Trixie bent down to pick up a large rock, but before she could curl her fingers around it, Charles dropped down into the cave. He landed with a thud on the ground next to her. The knotted end of a heavy rope struck him on the shoulder.

"Ouch!" he yelped.

"Quick, Honey," Trixie commanded, "grab the rope and let's get out of here!"

But Honey didn't move quickly enough. Charles reached behind him and held the rope out of their reach.

"Not so fast, girls," he said. "There are a few things we have to discuss."

"Really?" Trixie said innocently. "I don't think we have anything to discuss."

"Oh yes, we do, Miss Belden," he said menacingly. "Like the fact that you two have been snooping around me and this site since I first got here. And I know why, too."

"I haven't the faintest idea what you're talking about," Trixie said in her haughtiest tone of voice. "Now please, help us get out of here."

"Not before you explain what you're doing in *my* cave, looking for *my* treasure. For all I know, you've already found it, and have it hidden somewhere in here. You're not leaving until you hand it over."

"I still don't know what you're talking about," Trixie said sweetly. But she cast a warning glance at Honey. "Treasure? What treasure?"

"You know exactly what I'm talking about," Charles said menacingly. He began to shine his flashlight all around the small underground room as if looking for something. "I happen to know that there's a hidden stash of gold down here. Just because you two are rich, doesn't mean you can take it from me. You don't need it, anyway. And I'm not going to let two dumb, rich girls stand in the way of what I need."

"For your information," Trixie began, "I'm not rich, and . . ."

Honey, who had been listening quietly, suddenly stood up. She interrupted Trixie and started yelling at Charles. "You can't talk to us that way," she snapped. Trixie was surprised at Honey. She'd hardly ever seen her get angry. "It's not your fault that you're poor, and it's not my fault that my parents have money. You have no right to be so nasty. Besides, your dumb treasure couldn't be down here, because this isn't a cave—it's a cellar. Look!"

Grabbing Trixie's flashlight out of her hand, Honey directed the beam at the section of wall Trixie had scraped clean earlier.

"See? Nice square building stones—a cellar!"

There was a moment of silence. Then, to both girls' amazement, Charles's face crumpled. He began to cry.

Trixie and Honey were shocked.

"What did I say that was so bad?" Honey whispered to Trixie.

"I don't know," Trixie whispered back. "What do we do now?"

The girls stood still and watched quietly as Charles Miller's shoulders shook, and sobs of anguish came brokenly from behind the hands that covered his face.

Soon it was over. Charles gave a shuddering sigh and wiped his hand across his eyes. It left a dirty smudge across the bridge of his nose.

"What an idiot I am," he mumbled. "Now I have no money, and I won't be able to pay my tuition anymore. I had thought the gold would make it easier, make it possible for me to get my Ph.D. I can't go on like this, doing part-time jobs and being so tired all the time. I can't even study anymore. There's no time. And what's worse, my grades are going down, so I'm probably going to lose the small scholarship I have. I guess I'll have to quit school and forget about ever being an archaeologist."

Trixie could see by the expression on Honey's face that the kind-hearted girl was starting to feel sorry for Charles Miller. But not Trixie. She was feeling cautious. Maybe Charles Miller was deliberately trying to *make* her feel sorry for him. Was all this crying an act to throw them off the scent?

"I'm sure it's hard having to quit school," she began, never letting her eyes leave Charles's face. "But if you knew there was treasure down here, why did you bother to break into people's houses and steal paintings and silver?"

"Break into? Steal?" Now it was Charles's turn to be shocked.

"Trixie!" said Honey, horrified.

"That's right," Trixie continued. "I think all this moaning and groaning of yours is just an act. You're part of the burglary ring that's been breaking into the Westchester mansions —the Wheelers' house, too. I would think the money you got from selling all those stolen goods would be more than enough to cover your tuition."

Charles stood up with a look of complete dismay on his face. "I don't know what you're talking about," he said. "I'd never do anything like that—never in a million years. What kind of a person do you think I am?"

"Do you really want to know?" Trixie asked coldly.

12 ∗ A Surprise Suspect

TRIXIE TOOK a deep breath and squared her shoulders. Before telling Charles everything she knew, however, she decided to ask him to help them out of the old cellar first.

"I'll have a much better idea about the kind of person you are if you help us get out of here," she said quietly.

"Sure. Of course," Charles mumbled. "I wasn't planning not to, you know."

"We know that," Honey said reassuringly. She cast an irritated look at Trixie.

"I mean, why do you think I tied one end of

149

the rope to the tree up there before I joined you two in this hole in the ground?" Charles said sarcastically. "If I only wanted to yell at you, I could have done that easily enough from outside."

"Maybe we should let Honey go first," Trixie said. "My only worry is how we'll get Reddy out of here."

"No problem," Charles said firmly. "I'll go last, and I'll carry him in my arms. If I tie the rope around my waist, you two can pull us both up."

"I hope so," Trixie said as she watched Honey climb up the rope hand over hand. Using the thick knots Charles had made in the rope as footholds, she inched her way up and out of the old cellar.

"Okay," Charles said when Honey was safely out. "You next, Trixie."

"Gee," Trixie said as she started up the rope, "I'm glad I learned rope-climbing in gym last year. Who knew it was going to come in handy like this?"

As her head poked out through the hole by the tree stump, she took a deep and grateful breath of fresh air. Then she dusted herself off and called down to Charles.

"Now tie the rope around yourself and see if you can pick up Reddy." Reddy was jumping up and down excitedly, getting muddy paw prints all over Charles's shirt. Trixie knew the dog was worried they were going to leave him behind. "Don't worry, boy," Trixie called down to Reddy. "We're going to get you out, too."

Charles tied the rope firmly around his waist, then he bent down and gathered the squirming dog in his arms. Draping Reddy awkwardly over his shoulder, he held onto the dog with one arm, and the rope with the other.

Meanwhile, Trixie had checked to see that the rope was knotted firmly around the tree stump. Then both girls got tight grips on the knotted rope. They began to pull with all their might. It wasn't easy. Charles probably weighed one hundred and forty pounds, at least. Reddy was a sixty-pound Irish setter. Two hundred pounds all together!

But taking it slowly, and moving their hands carefully from one knot to the next, the girls were finally able to pull Charles and Reddy up the wall.

As his front paws cleared the opening,

Reddy leapt ahead. Charles managed to pull himself the rest of the way out. Trixie and Honey fell backward onto the ground, their arms aching from exertion.

"Whew!" Trixie finally said. "That was hard."

Charles dusted himself off, and said to Trixie, "Now, tell me why you think I'm a burglar."

Trixie, startled for a moment by the young man's worried expression, straightened her back slowly and then stood up. "I appreciate your help, I really do. But I'm still suspicious. There are too many things about you that don't add up."

"Like what?"

Trixie took a deep breath. "First of all, there has been a rash of burglaries in this area—all mansions and all in the last few weeks. So far, none of the burglars have been caught. Just last night, someone tried to rob the Manor House. But they got away with only the small Renoir. Maybe you remember it?"

Trixie saw that Charles looked upset, but she went right on. "The first time we met, you were very interested in that painting. You asked if it was real."

"I was merely surprised that anyone would have a real Renoir in their house," Charles began quietly. "I thought paintings like that were only in museums." Then he became more defensive. "Besides, I could not have been in Sleepyside committing a burglary when I was in New York City. I work nights, you know."

"That's what *you* say," Trixie said, "but maybe that's just an alibi. The burglars were interrupted in the middle of the burglary by Miss Trask. They accidentally banged the fender of their car on the oak tree at the curve in the driveway when they made their get-away. Miss Trask heard the noise. When I looked at the tree, there was yellow paint on it. That little yellow Volkswagen your friend Harry drives has a dented front fender. We saw it parked in the woods when we came here today. How do you explain that?"

Charles looked surprised. "There were no dents in the car that I know of," he said.

"Right," said Trixie. "But today there are, so the scrape is new. Harry is a friend of yours, isn't he?"

"Harry Kemp? Yes and no."

"And another thing," Trixie went on, feeling more confident in her accusations, "Professor Conroy was knocked unconscious soon after he'd spoken with you about letting us work at the village site. He thinks he banged his head on a low-hanging branch. But *I* think you hit him.

"In order to get him out of the way until you found your hidden gold, you made sure he'd be in the hospital for at least ten days. That way, as student head of the dig, you would have complete freedom to look for the treasure. And you knew where it was hidden because you found the map at the Historical Society."

"How did you know about that map?" Charles gasped.

"The same way you did—by looking in the archive room at the Historical Society. It was in Edward Palmer's diary." Now Trixie was starting to get angry. "How can you claim you're above stealing if you stole the diary? I even saw Harry waiting outside the Historical Society for you!"

"You mean it's missing?" Charles said, horrified. "I never stole the diary. What was Harry doing there?"

"How should I know?" Trixie snapped.

"And if you didn't steal it, who did? It's gone, and I saw you running off with it. I was looking out the window of the archive room at about three-thirty that afternoon—you know, the same day you went there with Brian. Didn't you hear me calling you?"

"Three-thirty?" Charles said angrily. "I wasn't there then. We went in the morning. You can ask Brian."

"Why should I?" said Trixie. "I'm sure you wouldn't steal the book right out from under his nose. That's why you went back to get it that afternoon."

Charles rubbed his chin thoughtfully. "I didn't steal the book. The big question is, who else would want Edward Palmer's diary?"

"But I *saw* you," Trixie said firmly.

"You only *think* you saw me. Let me think a minute. You say you saw Harry Kemp waiting outside the Historical Society, so it could have been Harry who stole the book. We can't be sure. By the way, he's not really my friend, he's a friend of Professor Conroy's. I didn't meet him until the day we were packing for the dig. And the Volkswagen belongs to Professor Conroy, not to Harry. You can check the registration if you like."

"And I suppose Harry was the ghost, too?" Trixie asked smugly.

Charles suddenly looked very shamefaced. His ears turned bright red. "Look, I'm really sorry about that stunt," he said, staring at his hands. "I wanted to scare you girls away from the treasure."

"Ah-hah!" Trixie whooped. "You admit it. I thought you were in New York that night, working at your job."

"It was my night off," Charles said sullenly. "I didn't scare you enough, though. You came back the very next day."

"Now that we have established that you were in Sleepyside the night of the burglary," Trixie said, "you could have broken into the Wheeler mansion."

"I could have," Charles snapped. "But I didn't!"

"Wait a minute, Trixie," Honey interrupted. "I just realized something. We saw the ghost at the same time the burglars were in my house."

Trixie pulled herself up short, then she looked at Charles. "That's true," she murmured, squinting her eyes thoughtfully. "One person can't be in two places at the same time."

"Am I cleared of guilt yet?" Charles asked harshly.

Trixie thought for a moment. Then she said, "No. You could still be involved with Harry, whether you were in the house that night or not. Besides, how did Harry find out about the gold if he's not your friend? You were pretty worried when you thought Honey and I were about to discover your secret. So why would you tell Harry?"

"Believe me, I didn't want to tell that weasel about the gold," Charles said bitterly.

"He was loading my stuff on the truck the day we were leaving to come up here," Charles went on to explain. "One of the cartons fell off the back of the truck and broke open. He saw my papers and notes. He said he'd help me look if I gave him some of the gold when we found it. And I needed the help. I knew I'd be working at the dig during the day, and at my job at night. That wouldn't leave much time in between. I knew that once he'd found out about the gold, he was going to help me look whether I wanted him to or not. So I figured that sharing it was better than letting him take it all for himself."

"That still doesn't explain the burglaries," Trixie said, pressing on. "If what you say is true—that the yellow car is Professor Conroy's, and Harry Kemp is *his* friend—then you're really accusing Professor Conroy and Harry of breaking into the Manor House last night. How do I know you aren't just covering yourself by accusing someone else?"

"I tell you, I'm not a burglar!"

"But you're saying that a close friend of the Wheelers—Professor Conroy—is a burglar."

"Wait a minute," Honey said. "Maybe neither Charles nor Professor Conroy is a burglar. Maybe Harry Kemp is, and the professor doesn't know anything about it."

"The two of them are very close friends, I tell you," Charles said shrilly. "Harry's in his tent all the time talking business, although I can't imagine what that business could be."

"That's a nasty claim to make about a friend of Mr. and Mrs. Wheeler, Charles," Trixie said smugly. "You know that Professor Conroy couldn't be the burglar. He's in the hospital with a concussion. He can't even get out of bed."

"Actually," Honey said quickly, "I don't think Professor Conroy is a close friend of my parents."

Honey looked a little embarrassed, then she

continued. "I didn't remember hearing my father ever mention him, so I asked Miss Trask. She told me that he came to my father with a letter of introduction from Professor Ingles at Oxford University. My father has known Professor Ingles for years, so it's almost the same, I guess. He didn't bother to check directly because Professor Ingles was in the Sudan on a dig, and my parents were on their way out of the country. But checking hardly seemed necessary. Professor Conroy was so nice, and he *did* invite all of us to join the dig."

"Whether he's a real friend or not is beside the point," Trixie maintained stiffly. "He's in the hospital. How can he rob houses if he can't get out of bed?"

As soon as she said those words, Trixie gasped. A disturbing picture had just popped into her mind.

"The shoes!" she yelped. "How could I have missed such a big clue!"

"What shoes?" Honey asked, perplexed. "You're always talking in riddles, Trixie."

"When I looked in on Professor Conroy this morning, I saw his shoes next to the bed," Trixie said. "They were caked with damp mud! That means he was wearing them outside, and very recently—like last night."

"That's right," Charles agreed, frowning with concentration. "And that's the one part of this mystery that didn't add up until now."

"What didn't add up?" Trixie asked archly. "I thought my reasoning was perfect."

Charles smiled. "It was. But since you wouldn't believe anything I said, I didn't feel like telling you that, as far as I knew, Professor Conroy was never unconscious. You told me that he said he banged his head at night, and woke up later in the hospital. That indicates he was unconscious.

"But when I spoke to him that morning he was fine," Charles continued. "He said he'd knocked his head, and that Harry was going to drive him to the doctor's office for his allergy medicine. But that was all. So when you told me about the concussion, it didn't add up."

"You're right," Honey said. "But why did Conroy make up that story and get stuck in the hospital?"

"I know why," said Trixie. "He needed an airtight alibi. Maybe he was afraid the police were closing in on him. If he is the burglar, we have to prove it."

"But how?" asked Charles. "Yesterday's airtight alibi is going to be just as airtight today."

Trixie began pacing up and down. "Just give me a minute," she said. "I think I may have a plan, and it just might work. But we have to get everybody in on it. That's going to be the hard part."

"Maybe we should go back to the clubhouse and talk it over with the boys," Honey said helpfully. "They could help us work something out."

"We'll go back to the clubhouse," said Trixie, "but I don't need any help figuring out the plan. I just need help putting it into action."

"What's the plan?" asked Charles.

"Let's go," Trixie said, picking up her flashlight. "I'll tell you on the way."

"*Now* am I cleared of guilt?" Charles asked again as they headed out of the woods.

"Let me put it this way," Trixie said with a laugh. "You're no longer my number-one suspect."

"That's a relief," Charles said. "You certainly know how to build a wicked case against someone—even if he's innocent!"

"What a thing to say!" Trixie said, bristling.

"I didn't mean that the way it sounds," Charles said reassuringly. "But I can just imagine what kind of case you'd build against a person who was guilty!"

13 * Trixie's Scheme

THAT EVENING after dinner, the Bob-Whites met at their clubhouse. Brian had been leery of coming until he heard that Charles Miller would be there, too. Trixie had asked Charles to come and help her convince the others. He'd managed to get the night off.

Trixie quickly explained her plan to the group.

"What makes you think it's going to work?" Brian asked. "It could take days."

"Knowing Conroy and Kemp," Charles said, "I think the plan has a good chance of being successful. Besides, what have we got to lose?"

Trixie was pleased to see a look of amazement cross Brian's face. He was obviously surprised to see how chummy his sister and Charles had become.

"I suppose you're right," Brian said with a shrug. "Why not give it a try?"

The next morning, Trixie's plan to catch the thieves went into effect.

Trixie met Honey at the foot of the driveway to the Manor House, and then they rode their bicycles into Sleepyside. Trixie was so excited, she could hardly breathe. When they arrived at the hospital, they immediately went to see Professor Conroy. After fluffing up his pillows and straightening his blanket, they were ready to begin. Honey pulled up a chair and sat down. Trixie stood behind her.

"I have something to tell you, Professor Conroy," Honey said. "I'm going to have to leave the dig."

"That is most unfortunate," Professor Conroy said. He seemed distracted, and uninterested in Honey's news. "Well, it's been very nice having you, my dear."

"I hope my leaving won't be an inconvenience, but it can't be helped," Honey went on. "My parents are staying in Europe longer than they'd planned, and Miss Trask and I are joining them there. We're closing down the house for the rest of the summer. I'm sorry. I know you need all the help you can get, especially now that you're sick."

The professor lifted his head from the pillow, and Trixie saw a look of intense interest cross his face. But he quickly softened his expression.

"It's no problem," he confided in a gloomy tone. "We might have to cut the dig short, anyway. This injury is affecting my ability to supervise. However, it certainly has nothing to do with you. Please don't worry about it."

"Oh, I'm so glad you don't mind," Honey said, pretending to be relieved. "I was upset about backing out on such short notice."

"Short notice?" asked Professor Conroy. "When are you leaving, my dear?"

"Miss Trask is packing now, and we're leaving on a 6 o'clock flight tonight. I know it's awful for you, but—"

"Don't think a thing about it, Miss Wheeler," the professor said with kind concern. "I hope you'll have a happy summer."

"Oh, thank you," Honey said warmly. "I'm sure I'll have a very happy time, and I hope you get better soon."

"Why, thank you," the man said. Then he sank back on his pillows weakly, casting his eyes to the ceiling. "I hope so, too. Now, though it's been lovely talking with you, I need to rest."

"I'm so sorry, Professor Conroy," Trixie said, hoping she sounded contrite. "Of course, we've tired you out."

"Not to worry, girls. I'll just take a short nap now, and I'm sure I'll feel more chipper."

Professor Conroy closed his eyes and let out a long sigh. Trixie and Honey tiptoed out of the room. They quietly closed the door behind them, and then ran for the stairwell where no one could hear them.

"Oh, brother," Trixie gasped. "Did you hear that? He fell for it—hook, line, and sinker!"

Honey could barely control her laughter. "We'll see if he did, won't we?"

The girls continued their rounds. The morning went slowly, but 1 o'clock finally came. With a burst of enthusiasm, they rode home as quickly as they could. Trixie ran into her house and found her mother in the kitchen.

"Moms," she said, "Di and I are going to stay over at Honey's tonight. Is that all right with you?"

"Of course, dear," Mrs. Belden answered. "Why, we'll be practically alone tonight. Mart and Brian just told me they're going to visit Jim at summer camp tonight. There's supposed to be a powwow."

"You still have Bobby to keep you company," Trixie said with a laugh.

"Thank goodness for that. I don't know if we'd be able to stand too much silence after all these years of a home filled with noisy children."

Trixie threw her arms around her mother and gave her a big kiss. Then she bolted upstairs and collected her nightgown and toothbrush.

"Where'ya going, Trixie?" Bobby called to her as she started down the stairs.

"To Honey's," Trixie called back. "See you tomorrow."

"You want to help me with my garden tomorrow?" Bobby shouted to Trixie. "You said you would."

Trixie stopped for a minute, somewhat ashamed. It was true that she'd promised

Bobby she'd help him. But so many things had happened that she'd completely forgotten.

"Maybe not tomorrow, Bobby," said Trixie, "but definitely the day after. Okay?"

"Okay," Bobby answered, a big smile brightening his face. "Day after tomorrow— and don't forget!"

"I won't," Trixie said. "I promise."

Trixie dashed down the stairs and out the front door. Honey was waiting for her outside.

"Next stop, the dig," Trixie said gleefully. The two girls headed across Glen Road on their bicycles. Trixie was whistling merrily as they rode.

Fortunately, they arrived at the dig during a lunch break. Trixie was glad. Now everyone would hear what Honey had to say. Harry Kemp was there, too. *So much the better,* Trixie thought.

Honey mournfully said good-bye to all the graduate students, explaining that she and Miss Trask were joining her parents in Europe.

No one seems very upset, Trixie thought. *I guess they never got a chance to know us, so they probably won't miss us.* But Harry Kemp smiled broadly—much more broadly than the occasion warranted—and he wished Honey a pleasant summer.

"Another fish," Trixie chortled happily as they made their way back to the Manor House. "Hook, line, and sinker!"

"We still have the hardest fish to hook," Honey said. "In the eyes of Miss Trask and Regan, this may be a crazy plan."

"Oh, they're bound to go for it. It won't be difficult for them, will it?"

"No-o-o," Honey said cautiously, "but I still don't know. By the way, where are Di and the boys?"

"Waiting for us at the clubhouse, of course," Trixie replied breezily. "Just where they're supposed to be. We're all going to lay this trap together. Ooooh, I can hardly wait for tonight!"

The girls' first stop was Regan's apartment. Honey told him all about Professor Conroy. Then Trixie told him the plan. "All you have to do is shut your lights off early and stay by the phone," she said convincingly.

Bill Regan looked at the eager girl with a puzzled expression on his face. "You know, Trixie, sometimes you do the strangest things."

"But it isn't strange, Regan. It's going to work."

"Knowing you, I'm sure it is," Regan replied with a rueful smile. "I don't know how you talk me into these things, though."

Trixie smiled. "Thanks, Regan. You'll see. This plan is foolproof."

Trixie and Honey clambered down the stairs that led from Regan's apartment, and headed to the main house.

"Now for Miss Trask," Trixie said excitedly. "I hope she'll do it."

"If she doesn't," Honey said, "the plan won't work."

"I know," Trixie said uneasily. "You'll have to help me convince her. Miss Trask isn't the kind of person who plays games."

"You have to admit, this is hardly a game."

"I know. That's the problem. I'm sure she'd rather call the police and let them catch the burglars."

"Maybe that's why she hasn't caught as many burglars as you have," Honey laughed.

The two girls went up the front steps and into the house. Miss Trask was just coming out of the library.

As always, she listened carefully and with

interest to what Trixie and Honey proposed. But she didn't like the idea.

"It seems awfully silly," she said, cocking her head to one side. "And you say that Regan has agreed to this?"

"He sure did," Honey said emphatically.

"All you have to do is spend the evening in Regan's apartment, and keep a lookout from his window," Trixie said.

"But how can you be sure the burglars are going to come back at all?" Miss Trask asked. "And why tonight?"

"Let's just say it's one of my hunches," Trixie replied confidently.

"Humph," Miss Trask grumbled. "It sounds as if I'm going to spend the evening sitting around in the dark, and all because I know how much you two enjoy playing cops and robbers."

"It won't be so bad," Honey said. "You can always talk to Regan."

Shaking her head, Miss Trask finally agreed. "I don't know how those two do it . . ." she muttered as she went back into the library.

Convincing Bill Regan and Miss Trask to go along with the plan was only the beginning. Next came Celia Delanoy, the Wheelers' cook.

Trixie asked Celia to make the Bob-Whites a picnic supper which they would eat at the clubhouse. Celia readily agreed. The night promised to be hot and muggy, and she welcomed the opportunity to prepare a cold supper and get out of the kitchen early.

Now the plan was really taking shape. By dusk, Celia and her husband, Tom, would be safely tucked away in their trailer. The Manor House would be darkened as early as possible.

Later, Miss Trask joined the Bob-Whites for supper at the clubhouse. When it was almost dark, they went to the Manor House and took up their positions. Miss Trask and Regan went to Regan's apartment. Honey, Trixie, and Di hid behind a clump of magnolia bushes just outside the French windows.

Brian, Mart, Dan, and Charles shut off all the lights in the house, and then hid. Brian and Charles stood on either side of the front door. Mart stood behind the huge double doors that led from the foyer to the living room. Dan hid behind the door to the library.

Then they waited. It felt like hours to Trixie. After all the planning and excitement of the day, she could hardly keep still.

Just as Trixie was about to give in to an attack of the fidgets, she heard the sound of tires crunching on gravel. She watched as a car slowly came up the driveway. As it rounded the curve, the headlights were shut off. Then the car continued slowly in the darkness.

Instead of pulling up to the front door, it continued across the lawn and parked in front of the veranda—only a few feet from where Trixie, Honey, and Di were hiding. The car doors opened slowly, and two men stealthily crossed the veranda and opened the French windows.

Trixie immediately gave the Bob-White whistle, long and low: *bob, bob-white.* She hoped that Regan would hear it. Suddenly the girls heard a yell and a growl from inside the house.

Bolting out from under the bush, the three girls ran for the French windows. Trixie gave the whistle again, this time loud and shrill: *bob, bob-white.*

Honey turned on the lights as they rushed into the house. The sight that greeted the girls was enough to make them burst out laughing. Brian and Mart were sitting on Professor Conroy's back, twisting his arms behind him. Dan and Charles were holding a large, blue-satin upholstered chair across Harry Kemp's chest, pinning him to the floor. Charles's knee was pressed into Harry's stomach. Both men had angry, red faces.

Moments later, Regan burst in holding a heavy wrench in his hand. Miss Trask was right behind him.

"Did you call the police?" Trixie asked.

"Yup," Regan said, brandishing the wrench in Professor Conroy's face. "I called them when I saw the car's headlights go off as it came up the driveway. Only an unwelcome visitor would pull a stunt like that."

It didn't take long before the scream of sirens was heard as a police car roared up the long driveway. Trixie gave a sigh of relief. She suddenly realized how dangerous her plan had been. The two angry men pinned to the floor might have been carrying guns! They might even have hurt one of the Bob-Whites in the scuffle! She was glad to see Sergeant Molinson come into the room.

He took one look around at everyone, then put his gun back into its holster. "Looks like you didn't need us," he grumbled when he saw how effectively they had subdued the two men. "I presume these are the suspects?"

"You presume right," Charles Miller said happily. Then Regan, Charles, and Trixie all started talking at once.

"Wait a minute, wait a minute," Sergeant Molinson finally said, throwing up his hands. "One at a time, and down at the station house. We need to take these two in for booking."

He shot a grim look at Trixie. Then he snapped handcuffs on Professor Conroy and Harry Kemp.

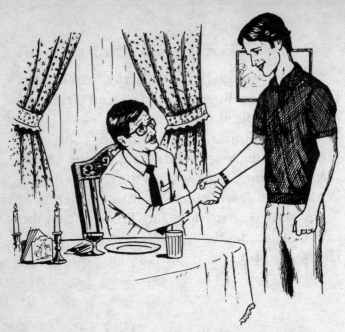

14 * The Real Treasure

"I CAN'T BELIEVE IT," muttered a graduate student after Trixie had explained the events of the night before. "If that doesn't beat everything I've ever heard, I don't know what does!"

The Bob-Whites were seated under the shade trees around the edge of the dig site. The late-afternoon sun shimmered on the meadow. But the usual feeling of busy activity was gone. Now the students just sat around, looking disheartened. They listened as Trixie told about the morning she'd spent at the Sleepyside police station.

"And not only that," Trixie added proudly, "it turns out that Kemp and Professor Conroy are the ones who committed all the other burglaries in the area, too."

"The thing I can't figure out," Brian said thoughtfully, "is how you knew the professor would come back to the Manor House last night."

"That was the easy part," Trixie answered. "I figured that after Honey told him that she had to leave the dig because she and Miss Trask were going to Europe, he'd figure that he and Harry could rob the Manor House in complete safety. And I had a feeling they'd act quickly, too."

"What I find amazing," Charles said, "is that Conroy wasn't an archaeologist at all!"

"He just wished he was one," muttered another student. "What incredible nerve!"

"Well, he was pretty good," Charles admitted. "He sure had us fooled."

There was a low undercurrent of grumbling as the students thought about how easy they'd been to fool.

"I can't believe how much trouble Conroy went to, just to get money for archaeological research," Mart said wonderingly.

"Sometimes the urge to be an archaeologist can be overpowering," Charles said with a sad smile at Trixie. Trixie smiled back. She understood what Charles meant.

"He pretended to be a friend of the family, too," Honey said. "And he wasn't even a friend of Professor Ingles."

"Conroy was just a clerk in the archaeology department at Oxford University," Trixie explained. "He took the job so he could get Oxford stationery, which he used to write phony letters of recommendation from Professor Ingles."

"He knew how hard it would be for the Wheelers to get verification from Ingles," Charles explained. "Remember, Ingles was in the Sudan, and very hard to get hold of—even in an emergency."

The young people sat in silence for a while, digesting the amazing events of the past day. Charles Miller looked around the dig site mournfully.

"And did you hear what Conroy said down at the police station?" he said. "He thinks he knows where the lost continent of Atlantis is located."

"What's that?" asked Di.

"Atlantis was a great, ancient civilization," Brian said. "We know about it only through the writings of Plato. It was supposedly destroyed by an earthquake, and then sank into the sea. Many people believe that Atlantis was a perfect democracy. Conroy believed that it was also a very wealthy land, but no one in academic circles would help him finance an expedition. So he got the money another way—by stealing it."

"I'm not a bit surprised," Charles said. "Who would spend all that money on a madman's dream? Of course, he could have made it all back—and plenty more—if he'd actually found some treasure."

"It sounds as if he thought he was Heinrich Schliemann," Brian said.

"That's true," said Charles. "Schliemann had absolutely no credentials as an archaeologist. All he had was a lot of money, and a good idea about where the ancient city of Troy was located. Academics thought Schliemann was a fool because he based his research on ancient legends, not on archaeological evidence. But he found Troy and really cleaned up!"

"If Heinrich Schliemann could do it,"

Honey said, "why couldn't Conroy? No one believed Schliemann, either."

"In a way, it's too bad he didn't get funding," Charles said thoughtfully. "It would have been fantastic to go on an underwater excavation—even if we never found Atlantis!"

"Now we should have a discussion about the lack of funding for worthy research," said a graduate student. "That's always good for a few laughs."

"You know what Mark Twain said," Mart explained. " 'Rich or poor, it's good to have money'!"

"What about the ghost?" Di asked. "What was that all about?"

Trixie and Charles exchanged knowing glances.

"A ghost?" Mart said. "How could you forget to mention a thing like that, Trixie?"

Trixie pouted. She knew Mart was teasing her about ghosts. "Oh, it was nothing. The night of the burglary, Charles was running around in the woods wearing a funny costume. He thought he could scare us. Hah!"

"It was a practical joke," Charles said, looking embarrassed.

"I knew there couldn't be a ghost," Trixie said as nonchalantly as she could. "So I decided not even to mention the incident."

"Not a ghost!" Di gasped. "I thought I was going to faint!"

"I wasn't scared at all," Trixie said smugly.

Honey coughed loudly, trying to cover her laughter.

"There's one thing I don't understand," Dan said. "How did Conroy manage to attend a burglary if he was in the hospital with a concussion?"

"Easy," Trixie said. "He faked the concussion. It's not so hard to do. The doctors kept him under observation for ten days, but that didn't keep him from climbing out the window after the last nurse check. They found the rope in his room.

"Harry would wait for him down below, and then bring him back to the hospital very early in the morning. He'd spend the rest of the day looking pale and sick. It was the perfect cover."

"Who wouldn't look pale and sick after being out all night!" Di joked.

"It was a clever cover," Brian admitted.

"And you know what?" Trixie added. "I bet they were planning to set Charles up, just in case the police got too close."

"Those beasts!" Honey exclaimed. "They were trying to make it look as if Charles were the burglar. How awful."

"Thank goodness it's all over," Di said. "What a week!"

"And what a day! We'd better get back home," Brian said, standing up. "It's getting late."

"We have to start packing up," said a student. "The dig is obviously over."

"Yeah," another student said glumly. "The dig is over, but the summer isn't. We won't be able to get any other jobs, and we won't get any course credit, either."

"What bad luck," Charles said. "The summer is ruined, and all because I answered a fantastic-sounding ad on the bulletin board at school."

"Maybe not," Di put in hopefully. "You never know. Maybe things will work out."

"I don't see how they could," he replied sadly.

"Charles, why don't you pack later," Brian said, patting his friend on the shoulder.

"Moms wants you to come back and have dinner with us tonight."

"Sure," Charles said. "I'd like that."

"Wait till you taste Mrs. Belden's wonderful cooking," Honey said. She had also been invited for dinner.

"Great," said Charles. "I haven't had a home-cooked meal in a long time."

The Bob-Whites and Charles said good-bye to the students, and walked down the road leading out of the dig site. Trixie could see that Charles was upset. She wished there was some way to help him.

For dinner, Mrs. Belden made her special hamburgers, potato casserole, and a big tossed salad with avocado dressing. There was strawberry shortcake for dessert.

Everyone was seated around the big dining-room table when Mr. Belden came in the front door.

"Hey, Dad," Mart said, reaching for a platter, "you made it in the nick of time. We were about to eat everything up. You know us!"

"I know *you*, you mean," Mr. Belden said with a fond smile at his exuberant and ever-hungry son.

"How was your day, dear?" Mrs. Belden said

as she took his jacket and his briefcase. "Sit down and tell us about it."

"I have a nice surprise," Mr. Belden said with a wide grin, "but I want you young people to tell me about your day first. I gather it was pretty exciting."

Trixie told him all about their morning at the police station, and everything that Sergeant Molinson had found out about Professor Conroy. There was so much to say, she hardly touched the food on her plate.

"And they found the Renoir in Professor Conroy's tent," she continued at breakneck speed, "and they traced the rest to a warehouse in Brooklyn. It was full of all the things they'd stolen."

"That's right," Brian put in. "Also, Harry Kemp had found out about a hidden cache of gold that Charles was looking for. He was probably planning to steal it from Charles, if he ever found it."

"By the way," Charles said, "did they ever find Edward Palmer's diary?"

"They sure did," answered Brian. "It's back in the archive room, safe and sound."

"But where was it?" asked Honey.

"Harry Kemp had it," Trixie said. "Apparently Charles told Harry that he'd found the diary with the map in the archive room."

"I had to," interrupted Charles. "He was pestering me day and night to get hold of that diary."

"Anyway, Harry wanted to see the treasure map for himself," Trixie continued. "That afternoon when Charles was busy at the dig, Harry went to the Historical Society. Jake Hanson told him that I was there, so Harry decided to wait in his car for me to leave. I guess he didn't want me to know he was interested in buried treasure. Harry saw me leave, all right, but I saw him, too."

"But I still don't understand why he took the book," Brian said. "After all, he'd made a copy of the map for himself. He didn't need to steal the book, too."

"That was just an accident," Trixie said. "After I was gone, Harry went down, found the book, and copied the map on his yellow pad. When he heard Honey and me clattering down the stairs, he panicked. The only way for him to leave the room without being seen was through the window."

"I get it," Brian said. "And as an afterthought—just to keep you and Honey from getting a copy of the map, too—he stole the book."

"Right," answered Trixie. "But he made one mistake. He forgot to take his yellow pad. That's how I managed to make a pencil rubbing of the treasure map."

"Oh, dear," sighed Mrs. Belden. "So many people think there's gold hidden around this neck of the woods. I've always wondered where they get the idea that hidden gold would stay hidden for very long at the rate people look for it."

Charles turned beet red, and looked down at his plate.

"I think you have to live around here," Brian said, seeing his friend's embarrassment, "to know how impossible finding gold really is."

"I bet Professor Conroy and Harry *would* have stolen the gold from Charles—that is, if he ever found it," Trixie said.

"You're probably right," Honey added.

"Well," Mr. Belden said, clearing his throat, "I think it's time for me to tell you what my surprise is."

Trixie clapped her hand over her mouth. She was so engrossed in her explanation of the day's events that she'd forgotten all about her father's surprise.

"This concerns Charles," Mr. Belden began, directing his attention to the silent young man at the end of the table. "Brian told me about your problem with tuition for school. So this morning, after I'd heard about the amazing feat you'd all accomplished, I decided to look into it. As an officer of the bank, I thought there was something I might do to help."

There was a long silence at the table. Everyone's attention was on Mr. Belden.

"I've cleared it with our loan department, and everything is all set," Mr. Belden went on. "If you'll stop by the bank tomorrow, I'll have all the papers ready for you to sign. We at the First National Bank would be delighted if you would give us the opportunity to help you finish your education—in comfort."

"You mean—you mean you'll give me a loan?" Charles said slowly. "Why, I don't know what to say. I don't know how to thank you, Mr. Belden. This is more than I ever expected."

Charles leapt up, and quickly walked over to Mr. Belden. Grasping the older man's hand, he shook it gratefully.

Unable to contain herself any longer, Trixie started to whoop. "Yippee!" she yelled. Her joy was so infectious that Bobby joined in, and they were soon followed by everyone else, including Reddy.

"This is definitely something to celebrate," Mart said, swallowing a mouthful of salad. "I'll have another hamburger in your honor, Charles!"

You see," Honey said happily, "everything worked out, just like Di said it would."

"I guess you're right," Charles agreed. "I came here looking for treasure, and I found the Bob-Whites, instead. Now that's a treasure!"

"And we'll keep on looking for the gold, if you like," Honey added. "If we find it, we'll give it all to you."

Trixie's eyes brightened. "We still have the map."

"That's nice of you," Charles said, "but maybe you should give it to UNICEF. I'm sure those children need the help a lot more than I do."

"You know what," Trixie said with a slightly pained expression, "I suddenly realized what this all means."

"Oh, no," said Mart. "Not another mystery!"

"No, silly," Trixie said with a smile. "It means that now we have to go back to being full-time candy stripers."

"And I'm supposed to believe that means no more mysteries?" Mart asked with a sidelong glance at his sister.

"Don't bet on it," Brian interrupted with a laugh. He tousled Trixie's blonde curls. "Where there's Trixie, there's bound to be a mystery!"